Saga of the Dead Men Walking

Slag Harbor

A Short Chronicle of Unpleasant Occurrences During the Search for the Coldstone, set between *Dead Men in Winter* and *Favorite Things*.

JOSHUA E. B. SMITH

Publisher: Joshua E. B. Smith
Cover Illustration: Alecia Gulley & Joshua E. B. Smith
josh@sagadmw.com

CONTENTS

YOU SAID IT WAS A TRILOGY!?

Technically…. yes, I did. I can explain this as "long story turned short."

When I wrote *Dead Men in Winter*, I expected it to be the second half of *Snowflakes in Summer*. When I went to go properly format the blasted thing, I realized that I had (almost) doubled the page count for what I intended to do, leaving me with (almost) enough material for a third book.

So, after crunching some numbers, I figured – okay. We'll make the Snowflakes series a trilogy. We'll go *Snowflakes in Summer* then *Dead Men in Winter*, to have everything wrapped up with *Favorite Things*. Except *Favorite Things* wasn't long enough on its own to publish as a third book without adding some material to it.

So I did.

And then I realized that the chapter I was adding had too many new characters and would feel completely out of place, but I had already written some twenty pages and I didn't want to just throw it away. So I pulled it out, set it aside, wrote a new-new chapter for *Favorite Things*, and finished the "main" trilogy and got it ready to publish.

That brings us here to *Slag Harbor* – the chapter that wasn't.
And since this takes place before *Favorite Things*, you're probably reading it first. So, just so we're clear: this isn't the end of the *Snowflakes* trilogy.

It's just a story of a guy sent to go clean up a mess he didn't make.

When we last saw him, Private Galagrin was ordered to stay in the City of Mud to make sure nothing unpleasant was left behind from the exorcisms of the day prior while the rest of Akaran's allies went to war in the mountains around Toniki.

Slag Harbor ties up a few loose ends left in Gonta and drops a couple of names for the novel to follow *Favorite Things*. Just consider it a short story going on at the same time as other, more important events, and you'll be fine.
Enjoy!

PROLOGUE

No war is ever fought alone, and no hero's tale ever gives
proper accolades to the ones that fight and fall in the mud.
Soldiers, however, are not always just those with swords.
Others bring Words of the Gods, some bring magic,
and some bring gold.

For every hero's tale, there is also a tale of a villain.
Just like a hero, they oft surround themselves with
men, women, and things that may or may not be noteworthy;
of course, to someone at sometime, they are worth something.

Nothing evil ever rises to power on its own.
Everything has an origin.
A deal, a mistake, a loss, a gain, an aspiration.
Of course, occasionally an origin becomes a leftover.

These minor players that are still so often overlooked?
What happens to those leftovers?
Do they fester, do they fade? Do they escape and come to power?
Do they stay forgotten,do they rise?

Sometimes a hero will sweep the leftovers off the field.
Sometimes a hero will ensure that which festers
forever rots in the ground,never to menace again.

Other times?
Other times, it falls to the ones that fight with a hero,
their own deeds important – even when forgotten,
even when never noted.

While war waged in Toniki,
leftovers rotted and leftovers festered.
Leftovers arose and leftovers menaced.

While the hero of Coldstone's Summit was busy,
a few of Akaran's allies grimly went to work to ensure that
those that rotted did so in the ground – instead of shambling on it.

While the Circle churned and the Plaguelord plotted,
his allies ensured that those that rotted
were swallowed in the mud.

Soldiers rarely see the results of their efforts. More often than not, they are sent to some misbegotten battlefield, given arms and armor, and granted permission to use them at their discretion. If they're lucky, they won't have to; their mere presence being enough to bring safety or carry a threat.

If they aren't, blood, pain, and death all follow.

Far too rarely are they so lucky.

So men and women take up arms, they clad themselves in armor, and they go do their bloody work. They get tasked to stick around for a short period of time, or at least, until the gore quits dripping. Then they are sent back home to parades and bards singing the tales of their epic victories. Or they go, and they fight, and bards sing a different type of tune as only a few return – songs more morose than monumental.

But regardless as to if they go and fight, or go and return victorious, or go and return with their broken bodies carried on their own shields? Frequently, they go and eventually return. They don't stay for long. They don't see the broken children laying on the battlefield. They don't see the sobbing mothers wailing in city streets, or the ruined fathers trying to drink away their loss, or wrecked siblings crying their names in empty fields out of earshot of anyone else.

Soldiers ever so rarely get to stay to bear witness to the suffering that comes from the wars they fight. While they may carry grief and pain and wounds of their own, it is far too uncommon for one to see what they leave behind. This holds true for soldiers that serve a mortal lord and or ones that serve a higher power – or both.

Exorcists are no different, and they may even be worse.

It's often they don't see the ruin they've wrought before they leave. Not even six hours had passed since a priest from the Order of Love had engaged in a whirlwind tour through the city of Gonta, excising one damned soul after another. He had been sent to the City of Mud to find an aspect of a demon haunting (and hunting) a village to the north.

Well, he found what he was after. After a bloody and brutal battle, Exorcist Akaran DeHawk tracked down a magical artifact of sorts that his quarry had hidden away in the city. Then later that day, he dealt with a *different* spirit that was working in tandem with the demon and had seen it sent screaming back into the Abyss.

But the battles were brutal.

And they were bloody.

Seven men, women, and children died. Five at the hands of the demon Makolichi, and one by the wraith Daringol (although the people that witnessed that fight would argue that Akaran was the one that swung the fatal blow, and they'd be partially right). One more person – a spy from the Civan Empire to the far north – had been caught in the process, and summarily executed for her crimes.

Nobody had enjoyed a peaceful passing into the afterlife.

Not all of them deserved one, but nobody got one.

Several of the corpses were burned outright in an effort to purify them on the spot. The spy was burned alive in her cell, though her corpse wasn't completely reduced to ash. Everyone's remains were packed up and carted (with varying degrees of care) to the Pyre of Ever-burning Flame for final disposal. The pyre stood a slight bit north of the city proper, nestled into the mountains that Gonta had been built along, on, and into.

Appropriate rites and blessings were placed on them in a process that took an hour for each of the unlucky sods that made it to the basin. Soon after, the appropriate remarks were said and sad noises were made, coupled with tears that were shed freely as they were consigned to be bathed in the fires of Pantheon. They were to burn for three days and three nights before their ashes would be collectively gathered and buried with (somewhat dubious) honors in the Sepulcher of the Lost (which was more of a pauper's gravesite than anything else).

As they burned, it was not unexpected to see mourners come and pay respects. Not unexpected to see a mother cry over her daughter, or a father come to give his farewells to his own. Although nobody there expected him, it shouldn't have been a surprise to see the spymaster in charge of the aforementioned Civan agent to come offer his own respects to a woman that he had loved.

(Though while he'd never know it, she used 'love' as a means to her own end – that was simply her nature.)

What was unexpected, and what was unwelcome, was the foul-smelling, filthy, emaciated cockroach of a man that watched the bodies burn from afar. Nobody gave him any thought and nobody looked at him for longer than they absolutely had to. Who cared if some ratty beggar came to watch the flames? Maybe he knew one of the victims. Maybe he was some homeless vagrant that just wanted to find a place to get warm (though if that was what he was after, nobody doubted that the Pyre's caretakers wouldn't chase him off soon enough).

He waited there until the wee hours of the morning, sulking in the few shadows near the pyre the whole time. When the caretakers excused themselves to change shifts, the wretch made his move. The moment their backs were turned, he slid out of hiding and skulked over to the flames.

The pyre consisted of a round gold brazier nearly ten feet wide and four deep that was set on top of a short flight of stairs under a white marble dome supported by four vine-wrapped pillars. Thin slats in the bottom of the bowl let ashes and bones fall out into a wrought-iron pan beneath to settle and cool. The fires within were enhanced by assorted spells that kept them ignited in perpetuity, and another spell helped the ashes and embers quickly cool once they trickled down into the bin below.

That lower basin was what the disheveled vagrant went after. Typically, a curator would ritually collect charred remains from the basin and deposit them in brass urns to be carted to the Sepulcher for internment under the grace of the Divine. It was all exceedingly, exceptionally respectful and handled with care – nobody civilized wanted to risk angering the dead.

The world had seen quite enough of *that* as it was.

Giving no thought for any of those concerns, the vagabond dug a small scoop out of the folds of his rags and went to work haphazardly shoveling them into a small canvas sack. Half of what he dug out ended up on the ground instead of in his bag, and when he had it full, he scampered off and ignored the furtive glances of the priests coming to start their vigil over the dead.

He should have counted himself lucky that he didn't join them.

There are men that do not care to see the remains of their loved ones defiled, regardless of the way or the why. It was barely tolerable that his charge-come-lover would be buried in *Dawnfire* of all places; the only reason he considered it even remotely acceptable was that her

4

body had been purified in a fashion befitting a Civan.

It was something of a sticking point for followers of the Goddess of Fire. Gods help them all if they had just decided to take her and just dump her into the ground. For that matter, the Gods should have been the only thing to keep Ralafon from killing the unwashed defiler when he caught up to him once they were safely away from anyone's potentially prying eyes.

In a way, the Gods did.

Or at least…. one of Them.

When their violent encounter ended, the vagrant was all-too-happy to show the Civan spymaster what he was up to and why he needed the ashes. A few hours later, and not only was the Imperial satisfied, he was willing to write off his lover's ashes as a way for her to get a measure of revenge against the Kingdom that had seen her burned alive in her cell. One horrific death deserved another.

And another.

And another.

Rmaci had accounted for several bodies of her own over the last month before being caught, tortured, and executed. Her remains inexplicably a part of a plan to account for a few more? In Ralafon's mind, that could only enhance her standing in the afterlife. Who knows? It might have.

It assuredly would help add to his…

I. SILTSTORM

The day before, Gonta had been the site of an execution by fire, an open battle of light and dark in the streets, and the unexpected appreciation of an exorcist from the Order of Love.

After Pauper's Row, the Temple of Light became oddly popular with the residents of Gonta. Apparently, seeing an actual demon of the Abyss rear its ugly head up and begin to kill people and claim their bodies gave everyone a sudden rush of faith. Although that wasn't the sentiment that Galagrin overheard muttered when he entered the courtyard.

"It's not faith if you've been given direct proof," the priest grumbled under his breath. "None of these faithless heathens cared before. I see little reason to humor them now."

"We humor them because it doesn't matter *how* they found faith, only that they have it now," a young woman quietly argued, reaching for his wrinkled hands.

The temple's Lower Adjunct snatched himself away and crossed his arms. "It is not faith. It is belief. It is belief in fact. Fact that *we* have, and have had, for centuries."

"If it is belief in fact to us, why not extend them the same courtesy? How often have we seen miracles of our own? How often have we prayed to the Gods, and they have given us Their boons?"

He glared daggers at the auburn-haired woman and into her hazel eyes. "It is our duty to channel the will of the Gods. We know it is fact because we had *faith* before we laid the first hand on a wayward soul. We would not have been able to bend our knees to Them without it. They would have rejected us."

"And these souls have had their own faith tested. Their faith that the Gods were relics and superstitions. Their faith that the only true evil in this world is within the hearts of their fellow men. Their faith that stories of unholy monsters and demonic beasts are just that, stories, stories that have a basis in wild animals and worldly creatures. Now they have seen a thing that is an affront to the Pantheon with their own eyes, buried their own kin, and heard of it from people they trust."

"But it is not *faith*," he protested. "It is not our duty to give up what we have for those that never wished it."

"They wish it now, Adjunct."

"Totoro, it is our decision to allow them entry or not. Few of them have done such a thing as to be worthy of it."

She frowned at him. "One does not have to be worthy in *our* eyes to receive the boons of the Gods. They must only be seen worthy in the eyes of the Pantheon. Let Them judge who is or is not to receive it."

"Our duty is -"

"Our *duty* is to provide aid *no matter to whom* and *no matter the circumstances.* When we begin to withhold that, we ourselves become no better than they; worse, as denying a soul a path to the Mount only condemns them to walk the path to the elsewhere."

He narrowed his eyes and straightened up to his full, unimposing height. "If you seek to infer that I am somehow less – *I*, after a trio of decades serving the Pantheon – that *I* am somehow less than that rabble outside, I will *remind you* that there are other temples in which you may serve."

Totoro smiled and straightened her white robe and calmly adjusted her collar before replying with a voice so soft that it would have soothed a rabid dog. "There are other temples and shrines, this is true. Yet you know how Deboria would feel if I found it necessary to move to another; I daresay that you would not be long to stay here yourself. She does have the authority to reassign us *both* – or did you forget?"

"She's the Priestesses of Stara. How dare you presume that I could forget what functions she serves in the name of the Mount?"

"Then I would remember to serve *your* functions before she returns. *You* may be the Lower Adjunct, but *I* am her handmaiden. One of us shall be easier believed than another, and even more so, given that if you order the others to withhold aid, she *will* know about it – and I daresay, as well as I know her, she will be less than pleased with you."

The Adjunct growled at her, then wordlessly turned and stormed off deeper into the shrine. Some poor page with unfortunate timing happened to be in his way – and became the next victim of his temper-tantrum. Totoro sighed and shook her head at the pair of them before turning to face Galagrin. "Soldier. My sincerest of apologies that you would have to overhear that. Not all of us are always so welcoming to changes in the way things used to always be."

Galagrin nodded and gave her an understanding smile. "I've had commanders like him. Letter of the law. Never the spirit."

"Never the spirit. What an apt description." Crossing her arms and then tucking her hands into her sleeves, she smiled at him as she studied his features. The boy – and really, he wasn't much more than a boy – barely had any hair on his head, with the exception of a short auburn goatee that had a single blue bead in it at the base. "Now with that done, how may I help you, Sargent...?"

"Private, m'am. Private Yolistal Galagrin, 13ᵗʰ Garrison."

"Private, m'am. Private Yolistal Galagrin, 13th Garrison."

"Private Galagrin. Welcome to our humble abode."

He looked around the room and raised an eyebrow. It was nothing but marble floors and walls trimmed with gold, silver, and the occasional streak of jade. Just to add to the gaudiness, it was accentuated with busts of various Gods made out of brass, onyx, and even shining steel. "I'm just a simple soldier m'am, but I can't say that this place looks humble to me."

Totoro laughed at that, her voice rich and full. "But it is our abode. How may I serve you?"

"I've been tasked with ensuring that the exorcist didn't miss any monsters before he left. Orders are from the garrison's vice-commander and the exorcist both. Priestess Deboria instructed me to come here and ask you to point me in the direction of someone named Inniat. She said they might be useful."

Her face crumbled a little. "Inniat? Oh. Dear."

"M'am? Did something happen?"

"You could say that," she sighed as she pointed back over her shoulder. "*That* was Lower Adjunct Inniat."

Oh, Gods, he groaned to himself. "I don't suppose it *has* to be him. Could be another priest. You all serve the same Gods, right?"

Totoro shook her head. "If the Priestess instructed you to find him, then it's him you need – not I nor anyone else. She has her ways."

"M'am, with all due respect, all of us sent to Toniki have had to deal with an absolutely awful old hag that's done nothing but give every single one of us shit since we showed up. Was truly hoping not to have to deal with another old codger intent on breaking a man's spirit." He looked at her and dropped his head. "Pardon the language, please m'am."

She muffled her mouth with her hand before her gigglefit could echo through the temple. "Old codger? Oh my – you *do* have a way with words. I completely approve of that; though I think it will be our little secret."

"Likely the wisest course of action, m'am."

"Especially since I'll have to have him go with you."

Galagrin groaned out-loud this time. "No chance I can dissuade you of that, is there? Or are you as stubborn as the exorcist?"

Flicking another grin at him, she shook her head anew. "I didn't have chance to meet the man. He sounds as delightful as delightful can be, from what I've heard. Now, please, wait here. I'll go fetch him myself."

Personal wishes be damned, she left him to stand in the glory of the statues of a dozen different Gods and Demi-Gods all staring at (and through) him. The entire experience left him rubbing his hands up and down his arms in nervous anticipation until finally, after what felt like a year, Inniat made his way back out to the foyer, grumbling all the way.

"Weren't you standing there when that stupid girl was trying to argue the nature of faith and belief with me?"

"Yes sir, I was."

"So tell me. Before I agree to go anywhere with you, what do *you* believe? Hm?"

The private gave a shrug. "I believe that if my commander tells me to go kill someone, I'll go kill 'em. If he or she tells me to go dig a ditch, I'll go diggin'."

The Adjunct looked at him with a blank expression. "What, praytell, does that have to do with my question?"

"That it don't matter why the guy needs killin', why the ditch needs diggin'. The Queen doesn't care what I think about their faith or their belief. The path someone takes to get to the end of my business ain't as important as the destination. They get there, and I do what I'm supposed to do."

"So you don't believe it matters why someone has faith, just as long as they have faith? Just like she does?"

Galagrin cleared his throat. "Sorta, sir. You got it right, too. They don't have faith right now. They've got facts. Bloody, shit-scented facts. They don't have *belief* as much as they have *knowledge*. Even still, *knowin'* a thing and knowin' what to do *about* a thing ain't always the same thing. That's when people come to people who can cope with it."

Inniat's frown deepened as he looked the much-younger soldier up and down. "Interesting stance."

"Just like what we're dealing with now. I know it's a demon. There is no question about it. That thing crawled up out of the pit somewhere and it keeps pulling poor sods into perdition. I *know* what it is. It scares the shit outta me."

"As well it should, from what I have heard of it."

"*Knowin'* about it doesn't mean I have clue-fisk-one on how to *deal* with it, except that I *know* there's people like you and that exorcist and that paladin up north, and the lot of *you* know what to do about it. So. I come to you, and then I do what you tell me to do."

The barest hint of a smirk went over the priest's lips. "And they say our soldiers are just blade-swinging thugs. I do see your point, though I'll confess I didn't quite come to it myself. "

"Oh, no, sir, we're thugs. Brutes that swing swords, get paid, fisk the occasional whore. Can't say that any of us are too special. It's what we do."

"So what it is *you* plan to do, knowing that there's such things as demons that walk the land, and that you now have knowledge of the place that they come from truly is a place and not just a hushed tale?"

"Fisk fewer whores, sir. Or find a God that I can pledge to that doesn't care if I keep doing 'em."

"A thug it is then," Inniat agreed with a wave of his hand. "Though you may wish to take time to seek out Makaral. I hear that He's very forgiving for that sort of thing."

Galagrin gave a happy little grin and bowed his head. "Thank you, sir."

Inniat cleared his throat. "Not that I could ever endorse such a thing, as I can only speak for the Pantheon, of which He is not technically considered a member. More of one of the Neutral. That aside. What is it you need, soldier? I presume it's not to debate matters of faith."

"Wish it were, sir. Got orders, and those orders involve you."

"Out with it; I do have duties to attend to."

"Well sir," he started, "that demon. It isn't working alone."

"Demons rarely do. They are demonic, and the legions of the pit are infinite."

The soldier blanched slightly and took a deep breath. "That exorcist yesterday. He's been after it for a while. I can't say I understand all of it, but there's another thing with it spreading itself all around. Now, Akaran thinks he got all of that one, but..."

Eyes narrowing, Inniat straightened slightly. "I do not believe that I like the way you say 'that one," he half-growled.

"Because there's others. Called 'em... what was it? *Shiriak?* Foulest smelling things you will ever run across in your life. Act like fisking rats, running about everywhere. Just... the *worst* things ever. He's afraid there might be more of them running about, or maybe another one of the Daringol spirits. Asked me to ask you to help check out the city."

"Asked me? I'm no exorcist. What good is it you think I can do?"

"Don't have a clue sir," Galagrin answered. "He said go hunt, told me where to look. That priestess with him, Deboria? She told me to come find you. I'm supposed to go collect another couple of men from the barracks and then go searching."

"I am an Adjunct of the Order of Light. I do not involve myself in dealing with... *foul-smelling vermin*."

Totoro cleared her throat. "You will make an exception to the rule, Inniat. If Deboria has wished it, you know you must do it. This boy couldn't have simply come up with your name out of thin air, so you know the instruction must have come from her."

Turning his head just enough to shoot her an evil look, the Lower Adjunct squeezed his hands together. "Is this your way of giving me another lecture on belief versus faith?"

"Can't say that," Galagrin interrupted, "just that I know what I know, and now I've told you what I know."

"How... quaint. Where exactly is it that you're supposed to take me...?"

The private held up the charm that Akaran had handed him. "Wherever this thing drags us, I guess. Though a bit odd. Swear I felt it heat up outside."

Almost as if on cue, a series of shouts made their way into the temple. One of the younger priests ran in and almost ran over the Lower Adjunct. "Outside! It's outside! They're back!"

Galagrin didn't even bother to hold back a groan as he gave up on talking and ran out to see what new chaos was going on outside. It wasn't too hard to find the source of the problem – he just had to run in the opposite direction as everyone else – and the amulet took care of the rest. By the time he arrived, his sword wasn't needed anymore, but that wasn't to say that there wasn't anything to do.

"Oh damn. I didn't want to see more of those," he said just loud enough for one of the guards next to him to overhear.

It didn't take all that long for Inniat to catch up. For an older man, he was surprisingly spry. "What... what *is* it?"

It was a yellow-skinned humanoid monster about the size of a malnourished toddler. Only instead of a human-like head, the cretin had a bulbous face with a trio of elongated jaws designed to open and close like a wilting flower. "That's one of those *shiriak*. Some kind of demon."

"A demon? Surely you jest. It's too small to be... demonic.

"Scavengers, they said," he replied with a shrug as his eyes started to water. "Not a threat on their own. Just... well. You'll see."

"I'll see what?"

As another one of the guards looked over at the private, he shrugged a second time. "Take a deep breath."

Inniat glared at him. "Take a deep breath? In Pauper's Row? I can tell you have never been to Gonta before, have you?"

Ignoring that, Galagrin covered his mouth and nose with his cloak and pushed his way into the throng of men near it (and gagging). "It's why my amulet heated up. Damn."

"This isn't worth my time. Look at it. It's so small. A child could kill one," the priest retorted. "Even I can see that. Those fools from the Order of Love always make things out to be much worse than they are."

"Just take a breath, sir. You'll understand."

"Oh, alright, if you do so insist." Glaring, Inniat took a nice, long, deep breath – and immediately turned green. "WHAT IS THAT?"

"Demon."

"THAT IS REPULSIVE!"

"Demon."

The Adjunct backed away and made a warding gesture with both of his hands. "By the will of all that is now and has ever been holy, such a thing cannot be natural. CANNOT."

"I said demon," Galagrin quipped.

"You said *demon*, you did not say spawn of a shit pile!"

"I didn't. The exorcist did," and then he quickly added, "Or, least, implied as much."

Inniat gagged around the smell and tried to spit it out of his mouth. "I can understand now why he sent you to make sure there were no more of these. Why is it he sent you to find me?"

One of the guardsmen – a corporal, by the insignia on his neck – tried to interrupt their squabbling. "You. You know what this is?"

"I do," Galagrin told him. Then, to Inniat, "Don't know, Adjunct.

Didn't then, still don't now."

"An insult, I am sure," he growled. "The Order of Love has long been at odds with the Order of the Pure. Forcing me to come witness such an offense is an act of spite."

"Order of the Pure? That's... Pristi, isn't it?"

"Yes, why?"

Galagrin poked at the beast with the tip of his sword and frowned. Someone had shoved a spear through its head and another blade into its ribs. "Well, maybe something this foul and this unnatural is something that your Goddess might take offense to? If She's all about purity, these fiskers are anything but..."

His eyes narrowed as he wipes his mouth with the sleeve of his robe. "That is... an interesting observation. We don't typically sully ourselves with the unclean, but for as much as this thing *reeks* I suppose an investigation may be warranted after all."

"Glad you think so sir, because much as I've dug shit-ditches, these are worse than anything I've ever had to bury after the fact. Even mom's beet-and-bean stew."

"I'm sure," Inniat replied, finally pushing his way to the front of the crowd. "Mayhaps Deboria had a righteous reason to task me with this... this..."

"Cleanup?"

"Private?" the corporal tried to interrupt. "If you know what this is..."

Ignoring him, the priest just continued on. "Apt choice of words. I will have to remind her that I am a Lower Adjunct, not some kind of... janitor."

"Join the army. You get used to it."

The only thing fouler than the *shiriak* was the look that Inniat gave him without even trying. "What was that?"

"Ah, nothing, sir," Galagrin quickly coughed out. "Well. Either way. Amulet isn't glowing anymore. Whatever it was doing here, it isn't doing it now. Still need to check out the cave that Commander Evalia found the other stuff in."

"*Other* stuff? I dislike this more and more by the moment, private."

"I do too," the corporal muttered. "Excuse me. I believe I outrank you, private; I suggest you answer me quickly."

Galagrin looked at the helmeted peacekeeper and offered an apology. "Yes sir, but I think the Adjunct outranks you, or at least, he outranks me, given everything that's going on. What I told him is the truth of it demon." Then, looking back at the priest, "Can't say I'm a fan either, sir. Still need to go collect Specialist-Major Badin."

"Another soldier? And what, do tell, is he a specialist of?"

"Battlemage, sir. "

"I am beginning to feel like this is all some sort of a joke. A priest, a soldier, and a battlemage all walk into a tavern…"

All it took was a shake of his head. "Trust me sir. Badin's no joke. Never met him, but I know *of* him."

Inniat rolled his eyes. "I suppose that will need to be seen."

"In due time, yes sir. Need to pass a word first," he replied as he faced the corporal again. "Apologies, sir. Afraid that I've got orders for you. Name?"

"Corporal Resig," the other responded. "And yours?"

"Private Galagrin, 13th Garrison."

Resig pulled his helmet off and rested it against his chest. "Since when does a private give a corporal an order?"

Beside him, another guard interrupted them. "13th? Evalia's company?"

"That's the one."

"Shit," the guardsman quickly cursed. "Corporal? She's the one that had Orin drummed out of the guard."

Resig didn't bother looking at him, but he sized up Galagrin a little more intensely. "Still doesn't mean he can order me around, Coric."

"She isn't that far from here; I can always send a message back to her," Galagrin offered. "If you want her personal seal and commentary."

Taking this as *his* turn to glare, the officer glared at him as the wind whipped a few strands of his black hair into his face. "What is it you want us to do?"

"Burn that," he said, pointing at the little beast. "Leave it where it is, and burn it to ash."

"That's not an order," Coric replied. "That's what we were going to do anyways."

"Gonna warn you. It isn't gonna smell any better when it's lit."

"Chipper," the other private replied.

Galagrin nodded in understanding. "Yeap. Anymore of those you see, get word to the shrine, me, or the barracks. Headed there next."

Looking down at the bloody pile of demon drippings at their feet, Resig sighed under his breath. "Right. Already sent a runner off to tell Captain Taes."

"Alright. Where did you find it, anyways?" he asked.

Coric pointed off to the other side of the canal at a pile of garbage. "Some urchin found it snooping around the trash. Scared it. It swam over here where we caught it."

"Okay. Thank you, Corporal, Private. Everyone else. I'll make sure those that need to know, know."

Resig kicked at the ugly cretin with his boot and grunted. "Who'd that be? The Overseer?"

"The exorcist."

The corporal's face lost a little bit of its color and he lost a lot of his confidence. "Same one from yesterday?"

"Yeap."

"Should the rest of us be worried?" Resig asked as he shied away from the corpse.

"Probably," Galagrin sighed.

"Chipper," Coric muttered. The other three soldiers overhearing the exchange echoed his opinion with varying degrees of profanity. "Absolutely fisking chipper."

Inniat crossed his arms and glared at the entire assembly. "It's so good to see everyone has the same feelings these days."

"It ain't the feelings," his not-entirely-eager companion replied. "It's the smell."

"Odors often evoke feelings, boy," the priest cautioned. "In this case, I feel ill."

And as they'd discover – so did Badin.

He wasn't the only one. Across the Row, a businessman in a horridly ugly coat that was just a few shades darker than a spoiled orange looked on with a truly unpleasant frown. Strumming his fingers on a billy-club attached to his hip, the portly fellow looked over at one of his taller, stronger, and slightly dumber, associates.

"You know, I don't believe I like that."

"Agreed, boss."

"I don't believe that I like that – a lot."

"Still agreed, boss. Think we should do somethin' about it?"

His boss rolled his eyes and sighed the sigh of the long-suffering. "No, I think we should let those ugly things rampage through the city, maybe feed them and keep them as pets. *Of course* we're going to do something about it."

His bodyguard winced and ducked his head. "Right boss, sorry boss."

"Question is, what. Did our mage friend ever come to a solid conclusion as to what that toxic chunk of rock was that we handed over to my new best friend?"

Running his fingers through the dark stubble on his chin, his associate thought about it. "Think I heard him telling Thadius that it was a mix of rot and ice magic of some kind."

"Well I can't say that there's much ice here – but rot? Now rot is another story entirely. Didn't the moron say he *found* that accursed hand down in Slag Harbor?"

"Yeap boss, he did."

"What would you suppose the odds would be that a chunk of unmelting ice that's tainted with frost and rot magic would just *happen* to be hidden in *the* place where half the city's butchers send their leftovers and a third of the farmers toss their scrap?"

The bodyguard nodded in quiet agreement. "I don't know shit-all about magic, but if something rotten is gonna be anywhere, the Harbor's as good of a place as any to hide it."

"Now I wonder – who would hide such a thing."

"That demon, I suppose boss."

"Ah, but if that demon had been the one to do it, he'd have been seen. This *is* a city of reasonable size *and* there are eyes everywhere. I know this, because I pay for those eyes. If one of these pustulent cretins had ever gotten near Gonta before, *I'd* know about it. No. It would have to be someone that lives here."

"Can't say I know of anyone that would..." he started to reply before his voice trailed off to nothing. "Well, maybe... there's that one... no, two..."

His boss quit strumming his fingers and affixed his man with an intense stare. "You're not as daft as Thadius. If you know something, spit it out."

"Well boss, just... until a few years ago, there was this pair of beggars, used to wander down on the east end, always smelled something shit-awful, like they were sleeping in the ass-end of a gutted bull. Never had any coin, just always begged for whatever passerby would give 'em. Used to chase them away on a regular basis. Then all the sudden, one of 'em vanished, not a word."

"East side of the city, you say? The side that's closest to the Harbor?"

"That'd be it."

The businessman cleared his throat and poked the end of his club with the tip of his finger. "What about the other one? You said two."

"Just heard he'd been spotted last night. Guess he was all kinds of distraught; made a mess and a half at Road's End. Rantin' about how he was never gonna get his lord's favor back now or some trash. Kendal was there. Told me he had to hit him in the face with a stool to get him to shut up and piss off."

"I don't believe in coincidences of this magnitude, Austilin. This foul-smelling vagrant have a name?"

Austilin scratched at his face for a minute and finally acme up with an answer to (hopefully) appease his boss. "Pegilu? Think that's it."

"Send the boys out. Go find this Pegilu for me. I believe that he and I need to have a bit of a chat. I have a *distinct* feeling that that soldier and that priest are going to be after him too. That's the same private that accompanied my new best friend when he came roaring through here."

"Can't say if he is boss."

"You don't have to. I can do that just fine." Akaran's unwanted *friend* from the day prior smiled and rubbed his hands together. "I want to find more reasons have him in my pocket, and I've got a strong feeling that it would be in the best interests for business if we make sure that soldier-boy over there gets what he's after."

His bodyguard gave him a slightly nervous glance. "Boss, you sure we should get involved? The army's involved, an' now the temple. May not end so good for us."

Raising an eyebrow, the businessman looked up at his loyal minion. "This city belongs to me. Whatever the Overseer thinks, whatever the Priestess of Stara thinks, whatever the old and new Captains of the Guard think, *I* own this city. It is *my* city. There will *not* be demons mucking about in *my* city or near *my* business."

"Right boss, of course boss, I didn't mean to imply that it ain't yours. Just that if they've got it involved, wouldn't us getting mixed up in it go kinda poorly?"

"Think of it less as a chance for it to go poorly for us, and see it as more of a *necessity* for our interests. Plus, if our interests become necessary for *their* interests, we stand to further entrench our standing in the city." He looked over at the now-burning *shiriak* and wrinkled his fat nose. "If a job is worth doing, it's worth doing *right*. I simply have no reason to have faith that those idiots can do it right on their own."

"Right boss, whatever you say. I'll get some of the men, and we'll go fetch him for you right away."

Riorik the Hobbler, Master of Gonta's Thieves, Guildboss of the Fleetfinger's Guild, narrowed his eyes and watched the small pyre briefly explode in a shower of sparks and yellow flames. "Make it a fast fetch. If there's more of those things scampering about, I'd like to make sure they're found before that smell makes me give up on wine."

Austilin gave him a quick short nod and took off running.

Honestly? He wasn't sure what he was more afraid of.

Finding another demon — or dealing with his boss sober.

Finding Battlemage Badin or recruiting him to the cause wasn't half as difficult as getting Inniat on their side. In fact, not only was recruiting him easy enough, Captain Taes was utterly delighted to have him taken off of his hands. "I presumed that when you stated we would be getting one of the local battlemages, that it would be one that could do more than just... reek."

"Hey. It ain't my fault," the soldier grumbled around the neck of a half-empty flagon. "Overseer had us marching down every back alley yesterday, lookin' for ghosts and demons. Name me one man that wouldn't set to drinking after that."

"We found one you missed," Inniat whined. "Not too far from the temple, at that."

Badin blinked at him through half-bloodshot/half-jaundiced eyes. "Sounds more like a problem for the temple than it does the guard."

Galagrin just smiled at both of them as they stood outside the barracks. "It is. Just not the temple you're thinking of. My orders are clear as they can be: make sure that there's nothing left behind that'll cause grief to the citizenry."

"You still haven't said what you think those things might be."

"I don't know," the private answered. "I just know where to go. Or at least, where I was told to go."

"You never did say where that was," Inniat complained, crossing his arms. "Should I spend the time to go back to the temple to pack?"

"No, sir," the youngest of the three answered. It was starting to give him a bit of a complex; Inniat was almost forty years older than him, and Badin twenty. "My orders were fairly pointed: Evalia encountered one of the wraiths with her squad about two hours downriver out of the east gate."

The battlemage balked and stepped back towards the safety of the barracks. "Oh, no. I'm not going back down there. I had to help bring back the people she lost."

Inniat had a similar reaction as he made a quick warding sign in the air in front of him. "Slag Harbor is no place for a man of my standing. You will have to find someone else to aid you."

Galagrin looked them back and forth and rubbed his face with the palm of his hand. "Look, sirs. Specialist, you outrank me. Adjunct, you probably do. Somehow. Listen. I've got friends right now that are up at Toniki, probably fighting, probably dying. I don't want to be down here any more than you. Or you. I've got my orders, my orders went to your bosses, and that now means I have to answer to them as well as my own. Sooner we get this done, sooner you can go back to drinking, sooner you can go back to preaching. Deal?"

Badin grunted and put down his flask for a few minutes. "You aren't from around here. You don't know what Slag Harbor is."

"Can't say I care, either, sir. If it's where I'm supposed to go search around, I'll go search around. If you refuse to come, you refuse to come, and I'll make sure that your bosses know as much when I get back to my bosses."

"Fine," the battlemage grumbled. "But you bring the shovel. I ain't."

The private sighed. "I'm a private in the army, sir. I always bring my shovel."

A short bit later, and he understood why it was such a necessity.

II. SLAG HAVEN

Slag Harbor was more than just a garbage heap.

The floods that poured through Gonta on a seasonal basis did a wonderful job at cleaning out the waste and refuse that naturally lined the waterways while generating additional rubbish from the occasional destroyed house, ruined crops, and drowned livestock. Less wonderful was the fact that the waters rarely washed everything downriver and all the way out to sea. Instead, half of the waste piled up in a natural pool a couple of hours to the south east of the city.

Never to let such an opportunity pass them by, over the last hundred years the city Overseers declared the area to be used as the garbage pit for the region. It served to keep the streets unclogged of trash, and, at one point, was home to the sods and slobs too poor to call Pauper's Row home. While the current wife of the most recent man to wear that title had ordered the area to be emptied of people, Slag Harbor remained the de-facto disposal point for all manner of trash.

It also stank to high heaven, a fact that Inniat had remarked on five times so far (and the battlemage twice). The only person that didn't seem to be affected was Galagrin, and that was only because he had worked latrine duty so often that the stench of all matters of decay didn't bother him anymore. "Just another glorious day in the army," was the only remark he had about it.

That inspired the priest to make a few remarks on the actual nature of glory, and an extra suggestion on what Gods he should consider serving. Badin simply laughed and took another hard swig on his flagon. When Galagrin drew his sword in the middle of their banter, they quieted and went on the defensive.

He hadn't seen anything; he had just hoped that acting like he had would get them to shut up. "Commander Evalia didn't say exactly where to go here. Gave general directions. It's deeper in. Said something about a cave on the far side of the harbor."

"If it's where she had us go a few days back, I know where it is." The battlemage stopped cold and planted his feet in the marsh as a thought dawned on him. "Just a moment. You don't know what's here, right?"

"I know what I've seen in Toniki. Wraiths. That demon in ice. And those yellow-skinned critters." He paused and turned around to look at both of them. "From what I hear, those ghosts can possess people and animals."

"Possess?" Inniat asked. "How so?"

"I'm not an exorcist, so I don't know how it works," Galagrin protested. "Just that they take bodies. Make them do things."

Badin couldn't stop himself from shuddering. "How do you kill one?"

"Akaran told us that the way to do it is to go for the head. Break their skull, it's gone." He blanched a little before explaining the *shiriak*. "Those small things? Kill them at a distance and don't inhale."

The priest gagged slightly. "Their smell is an abhorrence. Truly, an insult to all things blessed by the Divine."

"Is it worse than this?" Badin grumbled while waving his hand in the air.

"You have no idea," Galagrin replied, shuddering a second time. "Let's get looking."

While the locals called it a harbor, in reality, it was more of a marsh. Flotsam bobbed in semi-still pools of water, and you could see the odd animal carcass decaying in the reeds they walked past. Inniat punctuated every few steps with distressed utterances between whispered prayers. The battlemage kept his hands hovering in front of his waist, palms facing each other. Galagrin would have sworn he saw little sparks dancing between his fingers.

As it was, it wasn't entirely necessary. Nothing lunged out to attack them, and nothing spied on them through the piles of rubbish (aside from the occasional indignant rat). The amulet that the exorcist had passed down didn't even put off a dim glow. "Badin? You said you had to help with retrieval?"

"I did. Whatever went after them tore them in half. I lost a friend that day."

"Lead on?"

The battlemage rolled his eyes, fully recognizing he'd just walked into that. And then he muttered a set of profanity that would have impressed Akaran when he stepped in the mostly-submerged carcass of a long-dead dog. Those obscenities were quickly matched by their young leader when everything Akaran had handed him started to glow.

Inniat took the wisest course of action and stepped as far back as he could as the two soldiers took point and slowly worked their way through the muck. The closer they got, the hotter that the warding stones started to burn under Galagrin's armor. After another fifteen minutes of slogging, they rounded a corner and came face-to-face with a small earthen mound barely taller than an average human's height. "That's it," he told the other two. "Opens up on the other side. Don't know how deep it goes. The bodies were scattered in pieces out here."

"A horrible place to die," the priest whispered, distress showing in his hardened eyes.

"Horrible way they went. We're hunting the same thing that did that?"

"Gods above I hope not," Galagrin muttered. "Whatever our quarry is, it's inside."

Inniat shook his head. "I wish to remain outside. I'll be no good to either of you once we cross the threshold."

"Can you make light?" one of the soldiers asked with half a grunt.

"Excuse me?"

Badin looked over his shoulder. "Can you make light? I didn't bring a torch and I don't want to waste the energy. I might need it."

"Oh, well. I can. I am a Lower Adjunct, after all."

"Then you're coming inside," Galagrin told him. "Stay close, sir. I don't like this. This doesn't feel right."

The battlemage narrowed his bleary, yellowed eyes. "You feel it too?"

"Yeah."

"Don't tell your command. They'll send you to the college to do shit like I can do."

"And what is it you can do, battlemage?"

Badin sighed and took one last shot off of his flagon. "I bring pain."

The response took the priest off-guard enough that he was momentarily speechless, a moment that didn't last anywhere near long enough for anyone's sake. They also ignored his reply of "Well, I see how that could be a skill to cultivate in the army, yes," and instead needled him until he finally caved and began to work what magic of his own that he had.

It was a good thing that he did. The inside of the cave was as murky as the outside, and it quickly became evident that it went a lot deeper than anyone had anticipated. It was more of a shock that it wasn't completely full of water, despite evidence that the entrance flooded on a regular basis. The ebb and flow of light that slowly washed out of the priest's robes cast shadows away from the detritus for the first time in decades.

About twenty minutes in, the warding stones not only hadn't quit glowing and burning, they'd shifted colors from a pale blue to an angry yellow. When he complained about it, the battlemage had taken one of them and poked at it a few times with his fingers. "Did he happen to give you instructions on how to use these?"

"Just what he told the rest of us up at Toniki. If they glow, we're close to something we need to kill. If they glow a lot, we're close to something he needs to kill."

"And if the glow changes colors?"

Galagrin tried to wrack his memory over it. "He didn't."

"Typical for his Order. They claim to know so much, but they explain so little. And those things they do know are oft easily argued against with little care or thought," Inniat remarked with enough 'smug' in his voice to fill a Queen's bedchambers.

"You're not helping," the private whined.

"Neither did he," Badin muttered. "I don't think these stones are supposed to do this."

"What do you mean?"

The battlemage held one up and twisted it between his fingers. "The spell on this — I can feel it — is attuned to just one aura. The other one," he said, lifting up the second stone, "is attuned to a different one. They should not be reacting the same way to the same thing."

"It's just another spell cast by those fools of the Harlot," Inniat opined. "I'm surprised it even works at all."

"Oh there's nothing wrong with the spell," Badin countered. "It's rather ingenious. I wouldn't have given them this much credit myself, but now I suppose I must. You said that a neophyte worked this...?"

"Under supervision of his mentor, yeah."

The older soldier nodded and handed the gems back to Galagrin. "Mentor or not, I am impressed. If you could attune this spell to that of a human soul... the scouting regiments would be in heaven."

Inniat shushed him. "Let's not speak of death when we are in the middle of what feels more and more like a grave."

"It's not speaking of death when we're -" Galagrin started, until a heavy 'thud' and a rattling crash echoed out from deeper into the cavern. "Oh, *fisk* me."

"Starting to think we're all fisked," Badin grumbled. "We should go back for more help."

"There's no time," the private quickly snapped back. "That came from just ahead."

His elders shared a knowing glance and unvoiced opposition to his cockiness, not that it did any good. The soldier rushed ahead, shortblade in one hand ad a small handaxe in the other. After another short turn, Galagrin barreled head-long into a small chamber that made him come to a complete halt.

"Why is there a bed in here?"

Badin came in right behind him and nearly bumped into him. "Someone lives here."

'Lives here' was accurate, though to call the hovel a 'home' would be a disservice to the word. The bed that Galagrin had noticed stood at a slight slant, with one of the legs broken off. A table near it was covered in ratty pieces of parchment and there wasn't a chair to be seen. Someone had even laughably put down a rug in the middle of the room, though from Badin's standpoint, it could have just been a thin sheet of mold with delusions of grandeur.

The Adjunct was kind enough to point out the obvious without even trying. "What kind of disgusting troglodyte lives in a cesspit such as this?"

"One that keeps pets," the battlemage answered as he pointed up at a cage hanging from the ceiling. Or what had used to be a cage. Something had ripped some of the wrought-iron bars in half, and the occupant was long gone.

But it was still nearby.

It didn't roar as much as it did cry out with a screeching sound that *almost* sounded like a human voice. Galagrin had just enough time to bring his blade up to cover his face before the yellow and black blur came flying out of a side hallway right for his face. Curdled green blood splashed out from one of its twisting, snapping appendages as it bounced off of his sword and landed on the ground on all fours.

"WHAT THE PITS IS THAT!?" Badin shouted as the priest quickly backed out of the room as much as he could.

That was a *shiriak*, only… not. Black tentacles twisted out of a gaping hole in its chest, and oily, spindly black claws grasped at the air through a protrusion on its back. Tiny faces kept trying to push through its wide yellow eyes, and when it opened its mouth to scream at them again, Galagrin swore he saw another set of human jaws hiding behind its needle-pointed teeth.

Unlike other manifestations of Daringol's efforts though, none of these new appendages were ethereal – they were as real and as solid as Inniat's own arm. "That's not… it's different!" the private shouted, color draining out of his face.

"Different, same, doesn't matter," Badin snarled as he thrust his right hand out. "IT DIES!"

A bolt of lightning coiled down his arm and out through his palm. It struck the ground where the monster had just been, missing it cleanly, but kicking up shattered rock and small globules of molten dirt instead. Snarling, the battlemage called the same spell a second time, but only succeeded in destroying the already-ruined bed.

The *shiriak* rolled across the ground and launched itself up at Galagrin faster than anyone could track. It landed on his chest and dug thick claws into his chainmail, sinking deep enough to shred the rings and dig into his stomach. Screaming, he slammed back against the wall behind him and tried to batter the beast away. It ignored a thrust of his sword that went under its arm and out through its collarbone on the opposite side.

It scratched at him, one yellowed hand grabbing at his cheek as it wrenched his head back. One of the solid tentacles hanging out of its chest whipped at his throat, striking at him in a frenzy. When it managed to grab the glowing wardstone, the monstrosity screeched out a cheering cry that almost made his ears bleed.

"YOUR EYES – CLOSE THEM NOW!" As he stepped back into the room, Inniat used the only spell that came to mind to try to help the embattled private. "*Lumina, Lumina, cast shadows into nothing – cast all of your light into the dark!*"

At his call, the room nearly exploded in a flash of pure white light that nearly blinded both guardsmen through their clenched-shut eyes. The Daringol/*shiriak* hybrid had no such defense, and the blast left it screaming as it hung onto Galagrin's chest for dear life. The soldier grabbed the hilt of his sword and *twisted* the blade while pushing away, coring out the beast and finally succeeding in knocking it off.

Badin did the rest.

His voice boomed through the chamber louder than it had any right to be as he shouted his own spell, a single-word edict that called a bolt of lightning to dance from his right hand to his left and back before discharging into the cave roof. "THUNDERCALL!" Three quick streaks of electricity flicked out of his palm and licked the little demon across its face and down its back.

A fourth shaft of lightning burst out of the top of the cave and immolated the beast in a bolt that was easily as wide as the creature itself. The hilt of Galagrin's sword caught fire as the blade channeled the raw elemental energy deeper into the *shiriak's* jittering body. When the strike faded, the demon slumped forward – charred, smoking, and twitching.

Unconvinced that it was dead, the soldier staggered over, lifted his small axe high above his head, and brought it down with enough force that it cleaved the *shiriak's* skull in half. It quit twitching after that, and Galagrin slid down to his knees with his arms wrapped around his bleeding stomach. "I... I see why Evalia... had me ask... for you," he half-groaned through clenched teeth. "Gods. That fisking *hurt*."

Inniat cautiously walked over and assessed his ruined chainmail and took an educated guess based off of how much he was bleeding through it. "Well boy, I don't think you're dying, but we need to return you to the temple post-haste. I can only begin to imagine the number of diseases that a creature like... that... would carry."

"Time for the healers later, priest. Galagrin – is that all of them? Those amulets giving off any more warnings?"

He lifted one of the blood-soaked charms up and tiredly stared at it. "It's... still warm. Think there's more. Nothing as strong."

The battlemage nodded and let the sparks at his fingertips briefly arc to the ground. "Let's hope. That thing was... violent."

"Yes, it was. Too violent. That wasn't a creature that could be mistaken for small, simple, or harmless," Inniat complained. "The exorcist should have been here for that one."

Galagrin coughed and pushed himself back up to his feet. "Speaking of. Can we just take a minute and appreciate him? It just took three of us to put down that thing, and his type fight demons on their own all the time."

"Yes well, with the right training, anyone can use a tool. That's all they do. They just use tools," the Adjunct protested. "Highly specialized tools, of course, but still tools."

The private shook off Inniat's derision and shoved his boot against one of the tentacles sticking out of the *shiriak's* corpse. "This isn't right."

"You don't say," Badin said as he pulled his flask loose from his belt again. "Seems like another typical day on the job."

Sighing in not-so-vague annoyance, the priest started to walk around the room, small streamers of light still trailing along behind him to keep the room lit. "Only if you worked in the Fritan Guard," he snipped. "Not that Agromah would take a man like you."

"What? A mage?"

"A drunk."

Badin thought on it for a few and nodded in agreement. "So, what's wrong with that corpse, private?"

"It's still here," he answered. "The tentacles, I mean. The wraith. It's not... it's not a wraith. But it looks like it. Just... it's not."

"But it's dead, right?"

"Best as I can tell."

"So who cares?"

Inniat turned around and frowned at the two of them. "I will be the first to admit that I have no deep understanding of demonology, and I am happy to say that I am one that does not consort with the likes of those that do. Yet, in the many years I have walked this land, I have never heard a tale come to a happy conclusion if it begins with '...*and then the damned creatures began to behave unexpectedly*.' If you are convinced that there is something more wrong with what's at your feet than the fact that the thing that is at your feet is the embodiment of wrongness, then I would wager that showing care is not a poor decision."

"What he said," Galagrin added. "I haven't seen *half* the shit in Toniki that the villagers were telling me about. Some of those other shiriak. Then that monster in the ice yesterday. Now this. This is different than anything anyone talked about."

Badin flicked a spark towards a pool of water and watched it dance across the surface. "Well, it's dead now. Not like it's going to come back."

"Don't taunt the fates, battlemage," Inniat warned. "Galagrin: did that exorcist say if he believed that there were men behind any of this?"

"Not living ones, why?"

"Does this look like the home of a dead man to you?"

The soldier looked around at the ruined bedroom and shrugged. "I'm assuming dead men were living men once."

"He's got a point," Badin quipped.

"Yes, and an entirely unhelpful one. This... home... has been lived in. Recently, at that. Barring the unexpected I daresay the occupant may still be alive, albeit not necessarily here."

"Or he got ate by that critter," the battlemage contested.

The foul look that the priest cast his way could have curdled milk, had he the skill with rot. "If I thought I could bring you to as much ruin as this pathetic excuse for a mold-encrusted berth..." he started – and suddenly stopped as he reconsidered what he was saying. "Galagrin. Did the exorcist ever utter the name Neph'kor to you?"

"No...?"

Inniat's frown sank even deeper. "He should have."

"Why?"

He knelt down onto the muck and placed one hand flat on the ground, and another to his heart. "*Lumina, Lumina, show what shadows hide; show what casts them deep; show what blocks your light; show what swallows it whole.*"

Badin cast a nervous glance around the room as the hair on his arms started to stand up, and flinched as light began to pulse through the dank corners of the chamber, under the bed, and through some of the muck on the ground. Galagrin's body flashed once, briefly, and the head of his axe took a dim sheen – as did the battlemage's hands. The crest of Dawnfire's army began to shine a little brighter on both of their uniforms, and it gave the battlemage no comfort when a dull patch of light began to shine through his skin about where his liver was.

He looked over at Inniat (who was not immune to the glow – a faint shimmer of it settled over his head like a halo) and asked a pointed, angry, "What the fisk did you just do, priest?"

"Beseeched the Goddess of Light to expose the darkness in the shadows; the things that cast or cause death; the things that bring ill to the world." When he looked over at the mage, he pointed at the spot on his side. "You may wish to cease the drink..."

"Like he said. Dead men were living once. We all go out how we go," he replied as he took another swig and punctuated it with a disgusting short belch.

Galagrin looked down at the mark of Dawnfire on his chest and let his axe tumble from his fingers. "Okay, say that's the case. What's that piece of wreckage sitting over there in the water – and why is it lit up like the sun?"

Inniat stormed over to it, and took a long, hard look at the pile. "No... this is forbidden! It cannot be here!"

"What is it?"

"Badin! Call the strongest streak of lightning you can muster down on this… *blasphemy!* It is a thing that has no place to exist in this world, let alone this close to a shrine of Light! Destroy it *right now!*"

The battlemage looked over at Galagrin, shrugged, and thrust both of his hands out. Arcs of plasma danced between his fingertips for a trio of heartbeats before a raging storm of electricity jumped free and ripped into the wreckage. The impact melted it more than it blew it apart, and set the entire thing ablaze with Inniat standing right next to it.

He barely even flinched. Nor did he move away when a rotten green face briefly appeared in the cloud of smoke that followed the flames. "Be banished before the sight of the Gods, you horrific swine," he seethed.

Galagrin swore he heard the face laugh as it faded to nothing.

"Priest. What. The. *Piss.* Was. That?" Badin demanded.

Inniat bent down and picked up a broken piece of metal that the bolt had knocked free. It was a corroded bar of steel, twisted into a slightly round shape. "The Circle. You may not know of it, but *I* surely do. Nature exists as a cycle: things are born, they live, they grow old, they die; new life begins as their bodies provide sustenance for plants or animals – and the cycle continues."

"I can't say I ever thought that far ahead sir, but… go ahead?" the youngest among them encouraged.

"The Circle is a profanity. *Life* is growth. Not death. Not rot. Not decay. *Life* is growth. The Circle believes that life begins *at* death, not that death is merely a transition. But a beginning. That since all things must die, and life persists through death, that death is growth – that decay, that disease, that all manner of maladies are to be worshiped as a cause to bring the end of life so that more life can be gained."

Badin looked down at his hands as his mouth went dry. "That… that pile of rubbish. It wasn't rubbish."

"It was a shrine."

"To Decay."

"To the God of Rot. Do I need to spell this out for you at further length, or shall I assume that you understand now why I am full of such agitation? If the Circle exists in this city, and if the Circle is responsible for cretins like that sad misshapen thing, then it is impossible to know how deep this corruption goes."

Galagrin picked up his axe and settled it back in his belt. "I need to tell Akaran."

Inniat flung the icon back into the smoldering heap and wiped his hands on his vestments. "As much as it truly pains me to admit this, I would say you need to do more than tell him. If he's as talented as you've suggested, his presence will be needed. This cannot stand."

"Ain't just that thing, is it? What about the other stuff Galagrin's amulet is glowing about?"

"Let's hunt for it. Quickly," the priest muttered. "The sooner I can return to the Temple, the better."

Galagrin pointed past the smoldering shrine and towards a tunnel offshoot. "Only other door I see outta here is down there."

"Well. Isn't it nice of them to make it easy on us."

"If you say so," the battlemage replied with a grunt. "Galagrin, take point."

The younger soldier gave him a pained look and wiped blood off of his hands and onto his tunic. "Why me?"

"Because it takes me a few seconds to get the right kind of spell ready."

Inniat glanced at him and frowned. "The right kind? I wasn't aware mages like you had 'wrong' kinds."

The sigh from Badin could almost be heard outside. "Do you want me to just blow up one of those monsters, or cook the entire cave with us in it? The wrong spell can make things go badly."

Blanching, the priest stepped slightly away from him and fingered a pendant hanging from his neck. "I would be thrilled if you could wait to destroy the cave *after* we've had a chance to go through it."

"Then Galagrin goes first."

"You know what? Don't think I like either of you," he grumbled as he walked down the hallway with Akaran's amulet in one hand and his hand-ax in the other.

The specialist just shrugged and followed along behind him. "Mages. A General's best friend."

"A grunt's worst enemy, yes, I know the phrase." When both of the soldiers turned to look at him, he just shrugged. "My father was in the army. It is why I took up the cloth."

"Take it he had some war stories, eh?"

Inniat nodded at the battlemage. "He oversaw the transport of prisoners from the Privateer Wars in Ogibus. Some of the experiences he related lead me to believe that a greater good could be gained by helping souls find the Gods while they still lived."

"You ain't wrong there."

"Wrong or not, we're almost..." Galagrin started before coming up short just past a rotten wooden doorway. "What is *that?*"

That was a room not much larger than a small latrine and smelled just about as bad. It was full of cobbled-together shelves covered in filthy bowls and loose pieces of tattered parchment, to say the least. *Someone* had been doing experiments of some kind in here, and it was anybody's guess as to what the assorted piles of rocks and cups full of foul-smelling liquids were.

As for who or what the experiments were being carried out on, that question was easily answered by the makeshift cages set up along the walls. As Galagrin's amulet continued to glow, half of a man struggled to reach through the wooden slats he was buried under. The other half of it was nowhere to be seen, though his upper torso was doing a pretty good job at clawing at his prison – at least, it was doing good for being a dead man.

Nor was it alone.

A smaller cage had been braced against the wall, though to call it a cage was generous. It looked like someone had taken a wagon, set it on one end, and put chunks of wood on hinges on top of it. How it was able to stay in one piece boggled the mind; how it was able to hold a pig was another.

Both prisoners had faint tentacles sticking out of assorted open wounds and other orifices – little black tendrils of Daringol desperately trying to hold on to life. Both prisons had strange glyphs scratched onto the slats that flickered with pulses of gray light each time one of the tendrils tried to push past the bars. "Wardmarks. Whomever we're dealing with has knowledge of the arcane," Inniat muttered under his breath.

"Can you read them?" the private asked.

Inniat took another look at it and shook his head. "Read? That? I doubt even the man that wrote that could read such... chicken scratch."

"Would you give it a rest, priest?" Badin interrupted, sweeping his eyes over the monstrous experiments. "Not everything has to be an insult."

All he answered with was a barely-audible "Hrmph." After looking it over a second time, he shook his head. "Wardmarks. The only reason I can tell that much is because I once studied under Arch-Adjunct Grimbleb-"

"Don't care," the mage interrupted. "Those marks are what's

31

keeping those beasts in the cages?"

"If I were to hazard a guess, yes. Despite their state, I do not see these ramshackle restraints serving any good to *actually* keep them prisoner."

"Fine. Galagrin? Any ideas?"

The private looked back and forth between the pair of them and shook his head while he tightened his grip on his ax. "Ideas? Yeah, plenty. I ain't paid enough for this and the wrong people were sent to play cleanup."

"It's hard to dispute that train of thought," Inniat agreed. "So this cultist had a demon running loose in his bedroom, yet these things are secured and sealed up."

Giving up on talking, Galagrin went to work trying to figure out what had been going on here. While the priest and battlemage focused their attention on the monsters, he finally took a stab in the dark after finding a bucket half-full of *shiriak* blood squirreled under the table. "Well, whoever is behind it is... I don't know. Looks like they're... studying them."

"Yeah, it does," Badin agreed. "I'm going to take a guess that they didn't want that other beast to get out of its cage."

"Thinking you're right. Or maybe they did, and they just didn't figure out how to... domesticate? ...these two."

"Or they didn't want them to drag their stomachs all over the floor."

Inniat grimaced and squeezed his necklace a little tighter. "It isn't as if it would befoul it anymore if they did. Gentlemen, may I suggest that the two of you look for any kind of journal or scroll or parchment or *anything* that might offer a clue for what is going on here?"

"Us?" Galagrin asked, bewildered. "Adjunct, I think we'd be better off having a Justiciar or a dedicated squad from the garrison come to check this out? I wouldn't know what to begin to look for."

"Nor do I. However, it strikes me that as we don't know what was planned here, or where the planner has gone, we may not have a great deal of time to ascertain their goals."

Badin frowned and flicked a spark of electricity at the rotten man in the cage, just to watch it flinch. "Inniat, you're asking the wrong men to do this."

"History rarely gives glory to the right men, as they are rarely at the right place when they are needed," he retorted. "History tends to speak most often of the wrong men who attempt to reach a level of glory."

"I don't want glory. I want a bath," Galagrin grumbled.

The priest sighed and looked over at the pile of rubbish on the table beside him. "Then let history speak of you jumping into the river *after* we've searched this cave. When we're done, Badin?"

"What?"

"Let history speak of how a lone sparkcaster burned Slag Harbor to the ground."

The battlemage focused a bolt of mana into his palm and fired it at the pig. The energy was so hot and so focused that it burned the monster away into little more than bubbling lard in a matter of moments. "I can live with that." A small groan slid out of the other corpse Badin turned to it.

"See to it so *that* thing does not," Inniat ordered.

He was only happy to oblige.

JOSHUA E. B. SMITH

III. HARBOR TRASH

The trio returned to the city without further ado, and were by far and away happier for it. The sun was setting on the kingdom, though there was still plenty of light to be had. Which helped them walk in peace – everyone that even started to come near them looked at the gunk dripping off of them and quickly went the other direction.

The smell helped, too.

"I am still in awe you found a bag for that," Inniat stated as he watched Galagrin shift the dead *shiriak* mutation on his shoulders.

"I can't believe you insisted on bringing it back."

"Do not expect to be permitted to take that anywhere near temple grounds."

The private sighed at their continued bitching. The pair hadn't stopped from the moment they left the cultist's lair – and it had grown old an hour ago. "Not like we'll get to keep it in the barracks. It's gotta go to the temple."

Badin choked on whatever was in his (second) flask. "We? Fisk you. That's all yours."

"We. Army."

"I'm *guard*. Not army."

"Guard answers to army," Galagrin disputed. "Your barracks are mine. Regulation One-six-three."

The battlemage just looked at him incredulously. "You memorized that? No. I can still forbid you. Local guard still has authority to outrank transient army officers below the rank of sergeant."

"Gotta stick it somewhere," he answered. "Can't drag it through the city all damn day."

"No. Nor can you advertise it openly," Inniat conceded. "The city is already in the grip of terror. We claim more to this than yesterday's fiasco, and the populace will be further disquieted. It will result in unnecessary unrest."

The mage grunted and took another swig. "Disquieted. That's a word for it."

"You mean scared shitless."

It was Inniat's turn for a sigh. "I mean I've no intent to see Gonta riot."

They walked in silence down the street, keenly aware of eyes watching them from merchant houses, cramped homes, and darkened alleyways. "I know a guy," Badin finally said. "Owes me a favor. We can keep it with him."

"Is he trustworthy?" Inniat asked, locking eyes with a child that looked like he was about to rush over to them. With one brief stare, the kid quickly thought better of it and ran back into his house.

Sparks danced off of the mage's fingertips. "Everyone is, right bit of juice."

"I cannot approve of those methods, but I will not argue the results."

A flat, heavy voice behind them interrupted whatever retort that Badin was about to make. "You three won't need to. Come with me. Boss wants you."

Inniat turned around and glared at the thug. "Excuse me? Who are you?"

"Guy that was sent to bring you to his boss."

"I am the Lower Adjunct for -"

"I know. Boss knows too. Why he wants you."

It almost looked like the priest swelled up as he faced him down. Austilin outweighed him by a good forty pounds and half a foot tall — not to mention about ten years younger. The thug was built for just that; thuggery. Inniat, on the other hand, was anything but.

Not that it stopped him from exerting his authority. "I take my orders only from -"

Badin groaned and shut him down before he could make a bigger scene. "Inniat. We're going with him."

The Adjunct didn't let his gaze off of the brute. "Excuse me? I am going to do no such thing."

"Boss R.?" the sparkcaster asked.

"Boss R.," Austilin replied. "Hurry up."

An epithet slipped from Badin's mouth as he put his hand on the priest's shoulder. "Come on, Inniat. Galagrin. We don't want to be slow with this. Bring the bag?"

"With you, but not into the meeting. Leave it with the doorman."

Inniat stood there with his mouth open, trying to figure out why the wind was suddenly out of his sails. "What are you two rambling about? Where do you think you're taking us?"

Two streets over (not far from where they had reentered the city through the east gate), their coal-haired escort suddenly ducked down an alleyway between two nondescript houses. An equally plain but elderly gentleman in a white frilled coat nodded once at Austilin and opened a door into one of the houses. There wasn't any question about if they were expected to follow or not, yet they wavered for a few moments before the doorman placed his hand on the hilt of a sword at his waist.

"Swordsmen don't become old men just by chance," Badin warned.

None of them wanted to see if that was true.

Per the thug's request, Galagrin set his bag down and scooted out of the way while Inniat and the battlemage stepped inside. The swordsman looked back and forth between the private and the bag before wrinkling his nose and stifling a gag. "If that smell lingers in my home, I am holding *you* accountable."

"Don't blame me, your boss is the one that wanted us."

"My boss doesn't live here. I do. I have one mess to clean up as it is. Don't be responsible for another. Do I make myself clear?"

Austilin poked his head out and interrupted any hope for a reply that Galagrin could've mustered. "Yulric. Shut up. You, meatshield" he growled as he pointed his finger at the private, "get in here."

What was hiding inside the house made what they had found in the harbor look like child's play. A disturbed child, but child's play nonetheless. Four thugs were stationed at opposite corners in a fairly well-to-do dining room, though it was a hope beyond hope that the naked man stretched across it wasn't anyone's meal.

The thugs weren't alone. There was another man sitting in the shadows in one corner, and a slightly-portly man with chestnut-brown hair losing a battle against a receding hairline standing with a knife in hand over his unhappy, bloody guest. "This is unfortunately a most unpleasant experience. Remind me to avoid men of his ilk in the future,

Austilin."

"Masochist, boss?"

He shook his head and tiredly exhaled a deep breath. "Worse. Zealot. Not impossible to deal with, but not the most convenient."

The entire situation left both soldiers nervously clutching the hilts of their swords, while the battlemage began to pull some lightning into his hand – for a moment. Inniat, on the other hand, had a much more immediate reaction. "That man... he's been tortured? BADIN! Arrest him!"

Not that it did any good.

Badin took one look at Austilin's boss and bowed his head reverently. "Hobbler."

"What are you doing? Stand up man! Private! Do something!"

He didn't. Galagrin stood perfectly still, eyes going back and forth from one piece of hired muscle to the other, one hand clenching his blade, and the other pressed against his seeping gut. The Hobbler raised an eyebrow and smiled coolly at him. "Well, private? Are you going to do something?"

"I am sir. I'm deciding I don't want to be on the table next."

Chuckling, the so-called businessman placed his hand on the table and smiled. "Good man, I see. What about you, Lower Adjunct? You and I have matching interests today."

Inniat drew himself up to his full height and crossed his arms. "What possible interests do you think a man like me would have in a room full of thugs?"

On the table, the ratty, tortured sod started to murmur under his breath until Riorik covered his mouth with his hand. "Can't stop Him, you can't, you won't, He's... He's here in us, in all of us..."

"Another good man, and something of a wise man, I see," he said with a slight smirk on his lips. "Shouldn't expect less from a pious soul, though even piety has limits."

"Ones I am reaching," the priest warned. "Release him and us and I will speak on behalf of your kindness to the Justiciar."

Badin grabbed his robe and tugged sharply at it. "Inniat, *shut up*. That's Boss Riorik. *The Hobbler.*"

"I don't care if it's the Crown Princess. Release him."

"Oh, I plan on it. Directly into your custody. You two have a lot to talk about. Come closer, and I will show you what I mean."

The priest shook his head defiantly. "I will do no -"

Pushing at his back, Badin continued to growl under his breath.

"Inniat. *Do it.* I don't feel like dying today."

Glaring back over his shoulder, he relented and walked over to the captive. The sad piece of a man was little more than skin and bones with mangy brown hair and a mix of pox-marks and boils all over his skin. That, and the numerous open cuts and multitude of bruises decorating his chest and thighs. "You've done a number on him, I see. You wish to show off your work?"

"I wish to say it's all mine," Riorik sorrowfully replied. "A majority has been done to himself. Look at the inside of his thigh, just below that sad lump he calls his jewels."

"One would prefer not – but I assume I have no choice...?"

"You don't," the battlemage grumbled.

Inniat made a disgusted little noise from the back of his throat and complied – immediately before backing away, turning around, and shaking his head again. "I retract my statements. I don't want him. Keep him."

"It's rude to refuse a gift, you know."

"It is not rudeness to refuse detritus."

The Hobbler traced his dagger down and into one of his captive's cuts, eliciting a soft groan. "Detritus is right. I presume that it's been living in the Harbor. The shelter you found, most likely." Inniat's eyes went wide as he started to ask how he knew, but he was cut off before he could even speak. "Oh, don't be surprised. There is nothing I don't know, when it involves the city. *Nothing.*"

"I still don't want it."

Riorik shrugged. "That's a shame. Though you know, 'it' has a name. I would like to introduce you to Pegilo. I suppose he has a proper family name, but I can't be bothered to care. Pegi here is a loyal member of the Circle of Growth, so he says. I trust you understand how much that offends my sensibilities."

"Offends mine," Badin interjected. "His home? It's more like his laboratory."

"A laboratory? Well that's markedly more intriguing than I had given him credit for."

Inniat turned back around with his sneer even more pronounced than usual. "You can still keep him. I do ask that you consign his body to the temple when you finish your work."

"Was there anything of note in his den?" Riorik pressed. "Do regale me, Badin. You have my full attention."

The battlemage shuddered. "I've had your full attention before."

"And like then, I am sure you understand the import to express yourself quickly and concisely."

Blood rushed out of Badin's face as he took a deep breath and gave a quick overview of everything they had found, finishing with a couple of remarks on Pegilo's journals. "Just found several notes that he thinks he can do something with *shiriak* blood. Don't know what. You didn't find any vials on him, did you?"

Riorik frowned and pressed his blade deeper into the cut. "Vials? No, nothing as such."

"Yeah. We might have a problem then. Where did you find him?"

"It was quite a bit of a shock, really. We found him near Pauper's Row. He had soot on him."

Inniat looked down at the captive, slightly horrified. "He was near Pauper's Row? Near my shrine?"

"Not immediately near, but near. The graveyard, actually," he clarified. "Just past the Sepulcher of the Lost."

"A Circle cultist was found at the Sepulcher!? I will have it cleansed at once. I will not tolerate that... that... *repulsive* scum defiling the resting place of... of...! Even the forgotten deserve some measure of peace!"

It was Badin's turn to frown and it went deep. "I don't like this. This feels like a problem."

Riorik nodded and set his blade down. "Yes, I would agree. A Circle cultist performing experiments on demons and otherworldly spirits? While I am the farthest from a paladin as one could be, this doesn't strike me as a comforting situation."

"Comfort of the body is a thing you have a great deal of experience with, isn't it?" Inniat mocked (against his better judgment).

"Typically true," the Hobbler replied. "but I am also a man of reason. This doesn't strike me as reasonable, no matter how I spin it."

From the back corner, the other man spoke up. "So you asked the wrong questions."

Inniat's head whipped around as his eyes went wide. "I know that voice -"

"It would appear I did," Riorik agreed. "Pegi? Oh Pegi? Still with us?"

Glazed over and yellowed eyes looked up at him while drool freely dripped down his cheek. "Nothing can be done nothing will be done too late to be done..."

"Good, you are. I don't imagine you'd wish to speak openly without some more enhanced motivation, would you? Simple questions. What were you doing, why are you doing it? Things of that nature."

His voice started off slow and quiet, but ended in a shout. "Fulfilling a bargain; giving rise to new growth and glory!"

"Yes, well, while those are answers, they don't make a lick of sense to me. Anyone else? No? Then what bargain, what growth, hm?"

The cultist shook on the table and tried to pull free. "Bargain with the one that can't be found made a new one by one that found me!"

Riorik rolled his eyes and picked his knife back up. "I am oddly *positive* that will not be helpful. Gentlemen? It would seem I need some quiet time with our friend here. Austilin will escort you out and bring you back when all is said and done."

Gesturing at the door behind them, the thug didn't bother speaking – and the trio didn't bother arguing. Once they were back outside, Inniat faced the two soldiers and vehemently seethed at them. "You two are *absolutely* useless. That man is being tortured, and you did nothing."

"You told him he could keep the puke," the battlemage quickly pointed out.

"That was *after* I realized that he was our cultist. Even still, a trial must be held before the man is passed to one of the Queen's punishers, a title that I am sure that Riorik fellow doesn't hold."

"No he doesn't," Badin agreed. "He doesn't need to."

Galagrin looked at the grizzled swordsman standing watch down the street and interrupted their argument. "Who is he?"

"Just the most powerful man in the city," he answered. "You just met Riorik, the Hobbler."

Inniat shook his head. "No, the most powerful man in the city was sitting in the corner. I am at a loss to explain why Master Everstrand is holed up in that house of horrors."

That made Badin's eyebrow rise. "The city overseer?"

"One and the same. He was the one to remark about asking the wrong questions."

The realization made the mage shudder. "Well that's not good. Not surprising, but not good."

Inniat did his best to look down at the taller man without much success. "Would you please clue us in? Who is this Hobbler, and why do you seem to hold him in such reverence?"

"Can't believe you don't know him," Galagrin interrupted. "Even *I* know his name, and *I* don't live here."

"That's 'cause you're army. Half the army in this province is on his payroll," he said with a hint of a frustrated sigh. "Alright. Short version:

the Hobbler is the Guildboss of the Fleetfinger's Guild. Every thief, con-artist, smuggler, fraud, gambler, and whore in the city answers to him. Not kidding about the city guard. They get a nice stipend to look the other way."

The priest lost a bit of his bravado as he put the pieces together. "I... I see. I understand why that would give you pause to arrest the man."

"Arrest him for what? I don't know anything. Didn't see nothing. You see anything, Galagrin?"

He just shook his head and looked up at the sky. "I just see this damn sack and some building we stepped inside to avoid the rain."

Inniat frowned and stared at the private. "Rain? What rain? It's been dry as a desert for weeks."

He cleared his throat and pointed up at the clouds. "Our luck that it all cleared up then, ain't it? "

"Really is," Badin agreed. "I think we should stay here for a bit, make sure it doesn't start raining again."

"You know, me too."

There was no possible way to mask the scorn in the Adjunct's voice. "You two are pathetic. Men of the crown. Aren't you duty-bound to uphold the Queen's Laws?"

Galagrin pointed at the door and shrugged. "You're the one that said the Overseer is sitting in there. If he's trying to stay outta the rain too, I'm not going to say anything about it."

"I'm sure that the Master has his own reasons to entertain the criminal element of the city. I am not one to judge him," Inniat huffed.

"Good, then we ain't ones to judge the rest of these folk that are also tired of getting rained on."

Badin glanced at the sack and then rubbed his hands on his tunic. "I'm more worried about that cultist."'

The redirection worked to get Inniat to drop the subject of Riorik, though the concern in his voice did little for either of his companions. "Yes. Fulfilling a '*bargain with the one that can't be found made new by one that found me?*' That's a pile of gibberish unbecoming anyone, Circle included."

"Yeah, because they're such a threat these days," the younger soldier grunted.

"Your ignorance should be accepted for your age, though I feel inclined to correct you, private," the priest scolded. "The Circle is very much a public threat, and are actively hunted in every Kingdom east of Sycio."

Badin raised his hand slightly to interrupt him. "Well. Except for the League."

Inniat pursed his lips and gave him a slight nod. "Yes well, the Queen will see to it that the League is purged of Circle members soon enough. One can only hope she finds a way to expunge the ones in Sycio as well."

"Never did figure out why they were so welcome over there. Not like there's a lot of rot in the desert. Too damn dry," the mage added.

The priest just shrugged. "If Neph'kor had any sanity to Him, then we'd all be in much greater danger. However, that isn't to say that a cultist let loose in *my* city for Gods-only-know how long is *acceptable* and efforts *will* be undertaken to make sure that their corruption is banished from all corners."

"Got the feelin' that this is the kind of thing that'd piss off Akaran," Galagrin quietly pointed out as he blanched at the thought. "Seeing and hearing what he's done so far..."

"The exorcist? Yes, I have little doubt of that. I will send express instructions that he is to be dispatched here immediately."

"Won't be immediate. He's still got the rest of it to take care of up there."

"Yes well, whenever he's finished," Inniat replied with a dismissive wave of his hand.

Badin's eyes narrowed. "There's really more than this?"

"Lots more. And lots worse."

The battlemage chewed on his lip and let a few sparks dance between his fingers with quiet sizzling snaps. "You're headed back after... right?"

"Yessir. Gotta take that damn monster to him. Probably help him if I told him about the Circle, too."

"Aight. I'm going with you."

Galagrin looked at him like he just grew a second head. "You are?"

"The Circle is involved, right?" Badin asked. "And you're telling me things are worse?"

"Much worse," the private quickly confirmed. "That demon from yesterday is raising all kinds of pain up there, there's lots more of these wraith things, and a whole lotta walking corpses."

He made a less-than-polite gagging sound with a muttered curse after it. "Then it sounds like he needs all the help he can get. Inniat, agree?"

"I agree, it may be that he does. Or if not him, then the ones he is providing aid to. From what little I have seen of the man he tends to leave a wealth of chaos in his wake."

"Seems like it. Want to join us?"

The Adjunct shook his head. "You may find it hard to believe, but I do wish I could. This level of corruption needs to be purged at all levels, beginning where it is the worst. Sadly, I cannot. Once Pegilo is judged and disposed of, my immediate attention needs to be brought to the city – I dare not leave Gonta unattended."

Austilin stepped outside and barked at them. "Yer immediate attention is going to need to be brought inside. Boss is ready for you three chucklefisks."

"I beg your pardon," Inniat protested. "There is no reason to use such language."

Badin couldn't help but roll his eyes. "If there isn't now there will be later. Let's go, chucklefisk."

"Don't you even dare," the priest warned. "I am not one to chuckle *nor* fisk."

It was almost more than the private could do to keep his mouth shut, but he couldn't hold back a curse when he saw what was left of Pegilo. "For the love of the Pantheon, what did you do?"

Smiling down at his handiwork, Riorik gave him an honest answer. "I asked the right questions."

"You broke his shoulders and... how did you get his leg to bend like that!?" he exclaimed as he stared at the mutilated mess that the cultist had been left in. He was on his stomach now, with both of his arms twisted so violently that the shoulder-blades had separated. His right leg was twisted up with his foot shoved into his crotch, and then tied there to hold it still.

Pegilo, (thankfully for his sake), had passed out.

"So then. We had a discussion about where he's been and what he's up to. I daresay it's time for me to take a direct hand in this."

"Opposed to *what?*" Inniat thundered. "You call that the work of indirect hands!?"

The Hobbler started to frown and stepped away from his victim. "There's no need to use our outside voices, is there? As far as he goes, my mother always told me that I had a talent for tying knots. It's done me well. I didn't bring you back in here to discuss that, however."

Swallowing back his revulsion, the priest took his eyes off of Pegilo and did his best to focus on the thief. "Then what... what do you want?"

"Our new friend here has made plans to poison the water stores aboard the *Hullbreaker* – one of the Queen's battleships. It's currently moored down at the dock, preparing to leave tonight."

Badin's jaw twitched at the revelation. "Poison it? With what?"

"He wasn't quite so forthcoming with that," Riorik replied. "He kept saying that he was planning on 'spreading growth' with 'waters from the plowers of life's base' and 'dust of the shadow's passage.'"

"That gibberish could mean anything. But with everything else we found... anyone want to place some coin out on the idea that he plans on putting *shiriak* blood in it?" the battlemage grumbled.

"*Shiriak?*"

Galagrin pressed on the wound under his armor. "The ugly little yellow demons that have been running around."

"Ah. Proper names, and all that. I had settled for calling them bile-bags."

"Succinct," Inniat remarked. "The dust is another story. He was found coming out of the Sepulcher, you said?"

Riorik nodded his response.

It was the private's turn to clench his jaw. "When Akaran fought the big demon yesterday... a bunch of people died. How many was it? Half a dozen? More?"

"No, a bunch of people died and *came back* to life before he put them down a second time," Badin corrected. "With orders were to have their bodies burned. I know; I was there for cleanup."

"Which, one would assume, likely means that the 'dust' is the ashen remnants of those that were purified in Pristi's glory," Inniat added. "Somehow obtained from the Pyre? I'll have words with the caretakers at once."

The Hobbler slid his fingers up to the bridge of his nose and squeezed, clenching his eyes shut. "I have a third answer from his questions, though you will like it less. Before explaining, let me add this: the man we will be hunting belongs to me."

"Oh?" their gray-haired companion asked. "The cultist found a way to make use of one of your thugs?"

"Ah, no. You misunderstand. The man in question *belongs* to me. He was given instructions to vacate the city upon pain of... well, pain. He has chosen instead to meddle in the affairs of the kingdom instead, and that means he's chosen to meddle in my affairs."

"Can't have that," Badin interjected with the barest hint of a smirk. "Might have an impact on your bottom line."

Riorik glared daggers at him. "I do not need to have the city guard breathing down my neck, and I *truly* do not need to see a detachment from the army coming here to root out perceived 'traitors' until I am well and prepared for it. Which I am, at current, not. Thus, this man belongs to me, because he has suddenly decided to become a significant headache."

"Intend to strap a new body to your table? Lost in the underworld to never be seen again?"

"Oh, no, Inniat. He'll be seen. But yes, *after* I strap him to a table, as a matter of course. We're after a man named Ralafon; he is a Civan spymaster. I warned him to remove himself from the city or else his network would come under intense scrutiny. He has seemingly chosen not to."

Galagrin cleared his throat and raised his hand slightly. "Hold on a heartbeat, Boss Riorik, Hobbler sir."

"Just Boss will do, thank you."

"Hold on a heartbeat, Boss. How'd a Civan spymaster end up in bed with one of *those?* I don't know much but I've always long heard that the Civans truly have a deep-seated hatred for anyone that plays with Rot."

"More the reverse," the Adjunct quickly interrupted. "The Moldering God finds few ways to grow His corruption under the gaze of Flame. Thus, He oft takes issue with the followers of Illiya."

"Either-or," he quipped back.

Riorik looked back down at the cultist and thumped the back of his head. "A measure of ironic timing. As it turns out, Ralafon saw our friend here digging around in the ashes left behind from yesterday's *heated cleaning*," he started. "As it turns out, one of those ashen piles belonged to a Civan woman. Rala took umbrage with the idea that her remnants were being defiled by some vagrant."

"I want to feel sorry for his bad luck, but I don't," Badin grunted. "I imagine that he didn't enjoy the introduction?"

"Not that I was able to tell. One thing lead to another and Pegilo was able to craft a deal to spare his own life and give Ralafon a chance to take a small measure of revenge on the crown for killing one of his own."

"Shit. So the sonofabitch could be off at the docks now?"

The Hobbler pursed his lips and smacked Pegilo again. "Knowing that particular son of a bitch, yes, I would say that is a possibility. As much as I'd love to stand around and continue to chat with the likes of you, I'm dreadfully afraid that I need to go deal with this matter post-haste."

Badin drew himself up slightly and frowned. "You need? This is a military matter."

"I assure you, sparkcaster, that when I am finished with that gentleman, what's left of him will be handed over to the army; as will all of his other co-conspirators." Riorik flashed him a not-exactly-friendly smile. "My word on my mother's grave."

"Still an army matter," he argued as he crossed his arms. "Navy, suppose, but army in general. If you're going, I'm going."

"I can work with that but do understand – I have first claim."

From the corner, the Overseer spoke up again. "The military side of it will be overseen by the Overseer's office. I expect you to uphold your end of the bargain, Hobbler."

Riorik's eye twitched outside of his view. "Of course, Master. I wouldn't think of doing anything else."

"I suppose this is the point where you insist that I take this piece of trash off of your hands?" Inniat interrupted with a pained sigh.

"Oh, absolutely correct," the Hobbler replied with a bigger smile. "I cannot but help imagine that the Order of Light would like to open an inquisition of sorts into what exactly this little man has been up to under your noses."

"Unfortunate, yet true. I would also presume you'd wish for us to keep your involvement out of the review?"

Riorik nodded. "I would, though I am surprised you're making the offer. Does it come with terms I would have to agree to, or will you simply hold it over my head at a later date?"

"If you agree that you will work towards investigating your own ranks, I will do my best to ensure – though I cannot promise – that the Temple will only look into the spiritual aspects of the Circle's presence. Again though, I cannot promise it will stay that way, though I am not doubt certain you already have come to that realization yourself."

"It is a grim business," he admitted. "But I realized the moment that we caught him that light will be shed on the shadows. It will make my life difficult but at the end of day, there are limits to the type of corruption that can be tolerated, even in the underbelly of civilization."

Inniat gave him a faint smile and a nod of thanks before looking over at the corner of the room. "I assume, Master, you would like to be briefed on our efforts?"

"You'd assume well, Lower Adjunct."

"Shall I also assume that you *personally* would wish that the involvement of Boss Riorik is kept to as few eyes and ears as possible?"

The Overseer leaned back in his chair and flashed a grizzled smile at the priest. "And on the lips of none. I promise you that the Temple will be well-supported this year if so."

"Told ya," Galagrin quipped. "We're all just in here, trying to keep out of the rain. Just a matter of luck we're all in the same place at the same time."

Riorik chuckled at him. "Ah, yes. The rain. It is coming down in a torrent at times, isn't it?"

The cultist managed to crack open his bloody lips as his head dangled off of the edge of the table. "Rain, reign! They'll rain their reign down on you, it will be glorious to watch growth take to the seas!" he crowed.

Before anyone could stop him – not that they would – Badin calmly walked over and drove his fist sharply into his face.

IV. KILNFORGED

The Queen's Royal Wavecrasher *"Hullbreaker"* wasn't much of a battleship to the untrained eye. To the trained eye, she was even less of one. A *Legata*-class cruiser, she was at the lowest end of the navy's bread-and-butter.

At most, she crewed twenty men to handle her oars and rigging and another thirty to man fourteen cannons and a single *warballer* – a brutal piece of siege weaponry that was mounted on her bow. It could pivot to either side and was able to launch a variety of munitions at a foe; everything from explosives to incendiary rounds to even brittle iron shells filled with a toxic mist.

The latter was pure speculation, because what madwoman would be willing to use acidic gas to incapacitate her enemies? Surely not the Queen. She was calculating, but not mad. Or at least, so they said.

However, as a warship, the Q.R.W. *Hullbreaker* paled severely in comparison to the vast majority of the ships of the line in the Royal Navy. It was enough of a ship to serve in anti-pirate and anti-smuggler operations for this part of the province, and she was even called upon to serve as transport if the cargo was valuable enough. With a crew so small though, it confounded the Hobbler as to why Ralafon and Pegilo would choose to poison it instead of biding their time for a larger vessel.

That was until Galagrin quietly pointed out that if she was getting ready to be deployed again, it was possible that the poison was actually a contagion. With that thought in mind, the rest of the party quickly conceded that infecting a small ship would be a great way to launch a disease up and down the coastline, or even on to other vessels as the crew started to turn sickly.

By the time they made it down to the Port Authority, the sun had just about set with a few rays of light casting the river in a faint orange glow. Badin and Galagrin both felt like they had been running all damn day, and it was frustrating to see how well-rested their criminal companion looked.

The battlemage looked at the sheer number of fishing trawlers and merchant boats that were moored to the river's shores and bit back a curse. If there were less than thirty ships, he'd be surprised. Of that, no less than a third of them bore the colors of the Dawnfire Navy, and the rest were a mottled mix of merchant's guilds and local fishermen. "I'll notify the harbor guard. They won't be eager to let a Civan spy play about."

"It's not the spy that you need to be wary of, my good battlemage. It's his men."

Galagrin pursed his lips and looked over at the Hobbler. "You said we'd just have to deal with one man."

"Men like him hire other men," he answered with a shrug. "Do you truly think an agent trained in subterfuge would risk his own hide pretending to be a worker? Hardly. Far much more likely he'd hire someone to do the work for him; an unwitting dupe."

"Feels like there's a lot of those these days," the private grumbled.

"More given breath by the minute, sadly," Riorik agreed. "All the same however, while notifying the harbor guard will do little good, I'd think it might be useful to notify the captain of the ship in question."

The battlemage rolled his neck and shifted on his aching feet. "I'll do it. I've got rank here."

Riorik looked at the navy's line of ships and pursed his lips. "That would be the best idea. With luck, it will be enough to get you up the galley. Private? You and I will speak with Boss Mel."

"Who's that?"

"Mel – Melaine, really – is the harbormaster. She'll know who'd likely take coin and look the other way. For that matter, she'll know who'd take the coin and look at it dead on."

It was Galagrin's turn to nod. "Right. Lead on."

The thief's eyes went wide. "*Lead on?* My good fellow, do I look like the kind of man that goes somewhere with an escort and leads them forward? Badin..."

"Galagrin, go where he points you. Keep your sword out."

He sighed and drew his blade with a roll of his eyes. "Thought I'd get some time without taking instructions from everyone and their damn mule if the Commander wasn't here…"

"Hm? What was that, my good boy? I surely didn't hear a suggestion equating me with some kind of jackass, now did I?"

The private blanched and looked away. "Ah, no. No, Boss, you didn't."

"I didn't think I had."

Badin, however, just took a swig from his flask and stomped off down the river. "No, no jackasses here."

While there may or may not have been any in their little party, there *was* one standing prim and proper on the *Hullbreaker's* deck when the battlemage finally made it there. Captain Taes was a man that took himself far too seriously; everything about him screamed 'pompous prick' from the way that he had his red coat buttoned tight on a warm day to the fact that you could almost see your own reflection in the shine of his black leather boots. "Midshipman, why is this… guard… standing on my ship?"

The ever-present sneer on his lips matched the rest of his look perfectly. "I need to inspect it, Captain."

A pair of beady blue eyes went wide. "By what right does some pissant guard think he has to *inspect* my ship, let alone board it without my express permission?'"

"One that can scuttle your ship if you push the issue."

"*EXCUSE ME!?* SCUTTLE? Just who do you think you are?"

"A Specialist-Major attached to the guard, on loan from Maiden Piata's Consort," he shot back. "Battlemage designation; and specifically? A sparkcaster. And your ship looks like it hasn't been struck by lightning recently. Now let's talk."

Taes stepped right up to his face and snarled into his face. "I am a commander of a royal navy vessel, and you come on board to *threaten* me? I should have you tossed into the brig and thrown overboard once we're at sea."

Badin sighed and stepped back to keep from punching him. "Maybe you can tone the bluster down once I tell you why I'm here. The Guard has been made aware of a threat against a navy ship – *this* ship. Poison is the suspected threat; possibly already on board."

"Poison? Some fool intends to… are you mad, boy? If there's such a threat, we'd have heard about it by now! We're to lift anchor within the hour!"

"It's easier to warn you now than warn you after you set sail," he retorted. "Now, I need to inspect your ship. Not entirely sure what I'm looking for, but I gotta look anyways."

"You don't even know what this supposed poison looks like?" Taes scoffed.

He shrugged and looked at everything but the captain. "Well, given the fact that the thing that makes it bleeds yellow, thought that might be a good start."

"The thing that makes it? You're speaking a load of gibberish."

"With all due respect Captain, just shut up and listen. We found a cultist that claims allegiance to the Plaguelord. Bastard has been milking some awful little creatures for their blood; we've got a priest that says they're pitborn. Same sack of shit said he was gonna try and do some damage against the queen."

Taes' outrage died down some as he pursed his lips. "That's quite a tale. Do you expect me to believe that there are demons running around the city unchecked?"

"By this point, we're confident they're checked. I'm assuming you heard about yesterday's cockup?"

He crossed his arms and frowned. "That 'cockup,' as you put it, is why we are being dispatched from port early. In the event of another attack, *your* commanders have made a request that we have soldiers off-land to serve as emergency relief. Once that's been done, we have orders to travel elsewhere."

"Sounds right for them. Now, let me search."

"How exactly am I to believe that you aren't the poisoner?"

Badin's jaw opened but he couldn't quite get a sound out of his mouth for the longest time. "What did you just say?"

"You come here with these wild accusations, say you're looking for a poison that you think *might* be yellow, you don't know where it would be applied," Taes argued. "Am I to assume you don't know what it does?"

"Not a clue. Figured 'demon blood' was about all I needed to care about."

"Well that might work just fine for you," he retorted with a sneer. "but I did not become captain of a *Legata*-class ship by not understanding the keenest of details in all things."

"Yeah. I'm *sure* that's the reason you became captain of a ship this size."

Two of the sailors listening to the exchange behind the captain coughed, and a third made a quiet spluttering sound behind his flagon.

"Be sure of anything you like. Your request is *denied*, guardsman. I will have my men search the ship once we're set off."

"Are you kidding me? I just told you that you might be carrying around -"

Taes got in his face again and smirked. "Yes, I heard you. Do you think you, just one man, are somehow better equipped to search for this mythical substance than an entire ship full of the Queen's men?"

"Yes."

"Then I shall have someone notify your commanding officer that your ego runs unchecked."

"He knows."

The captain glared at him and pointed back down to the docks. "You may remove yourself from my ship at once. If, and I sincerely doubt that we will, *if* we find any evidence that your worries are somehow true, I will make sure that your superiors are notified."

"You're on a ship!" Badin shouted. "By the time you find out, you'll probably already be at sea, and unless things have changed, the Queen won't have you sailing going up and down the river just so you can end up back here. That means your next port-of-call is days or weeks away, at best, and by then it won't matter to anyone but the undertakers if you're right or not."

"Then you will have to trust that we will deal with it and that the Holy General will be provided a record of our work," he retorted.

Sparks flashed off of his fingertips and scored little black marks on the chainmail over his thighs. "You're being an idiot, *Captain*."

"And *you* are being an insubordinate drunk. Yes, battlemage, I can smell it on your breath."

"I'm not drunk," he snapped back. "Been drinking, but not drunk. You'd be drinking if you'd seen half the shit I've seen today."

"The majority of which are hallucinations brought about by a failing liver, I am quite sure. Now remove yourself from my ship or I will have my men do it for you."

Badin backed off and turned around, stomping down the gangplank. "Yeah, fine. Whatever. You report this to your bosses, I'll report it to mine. For the sake of your men, you'd better hope I'm wrong. I've *seen* the things that this blood comes out of. You *don't* want to drink from them."

"I am positive that will not be an issue for us," Taes shouted back. "Now go!"

While Badin was being escorted off of the *Hullbreaker* by two overly-burly and ill-amused sailors, Riorik and his newest 'Why me?' friend were getting an entirely different reception from Boss Mel. "Wouldn't surprise me none if it turned out that some of these boys were bought by the Empire. Pits, wouldn't surprise me none of one of these worthless shits were *from* the Empire."

"That's a tad more pessimistic than your normally shiny outlook," Riorik replied with a slight grin on his rounded cheeks. "Are we having trouble in paradise?"

Mel, Galagrin decided, was the type of woman that would make you melt with her sky-blue eyes, wrap the end of her fingers up in her auburn hair, and then beat you to death with an oar just because she felt like it. "Paradise? *Paradise?* Does it appear to you that this putrid pisspot is some kind of *paradise?*"

Flashing her a smile – and not backing down an inch as she towered over him – the Hobbler turned up the charm. "Oh you must be having a day. Tell me, what troubles a lady fine as you?"

The private wished he didn't have to. "Boss Hobbler, we don't have time for this."

"There's always time to talk to a pretty woman. I am surprised you're not taught this in your training."

"By my father, but -"

Riorik took her hand in his and absolutely oozed charisma from his every pore. "So what troubles you, Mel? Too many shipments coming from the west? Too many refugees trying to get out?"

She pulled her hand back and looked out of her office and down at the harbor below. "All that shit and more. That fisking ship of the line down there is the *third* one this month, and they keep mucking shit up out there. I've got Blackstone-hired cargo haulers loading *sylverine* every fisking hour. Top that with the fools trying to run away thinking that the Abyss has started puking up its most rotten, and you bet your ass I've got headaches."

"It does sound like it. I am sorry about your troubles, but I am afraid that my matter is most urgent and needs to preempt all of your other concerns."

Mel sat down and sighed. In the lamplight, Galagrin could count every single one of the wrinkles around her eyes. "Yeah well. Half these slags would sell their mother for the promise of old ale and a sloppy cocksuck from a whore with blistered lips. Just spiking the ale stores of a Queen's vessel? There's no love for the navy here."

"Not getting the feeling that there's much love for the army, either," the private quipped.

"The army? Well now, that's a different story. Plenty of love for the army down here. Granted, you'll pay twice what the rest of us have to, but there's still plenty."

She looked up at him with a mischievous glint in her eyes that made him feel like he was being actively hunted. "Think I'll have to pass this time out, m'am," he half-stuttered.

"Your loss, boy. I can recommend a few. As for you, Boss Hob, I can rattle off five names that'd be happy to do the job you're suggesting."

Riorik winced and waved his hand at her. "Please, madam, do not call me 'Boss Hob.' I believe we talked about that once before."

"Twice, but I'll let you know if I decide to actually quit doing it."

"Decide to quit doing it, please."

Smiling at his discomfort, Mel stretched and leaned back in her chair. "Now I don't think that me using just three little letters is enough to warrant losing access to my docks, now is it?"

He looked down at his feet and grumbled something impolite before speaking up. "It might be worth you losing the ability to *walk*."

"If I can't walk, your goods can't sail," she reminded him. "Now. Like I said. I can give you five men, but if you're adamant that the attack'll happen today, only two men would've gotten to that side of the docks without raising suspicions."

"I wouldn't suppose you'd know off hand who that would be?"

She ignored him and shouted out the window at a passing dockworker. "Hey, Kelchen. Go find me Wallgon and Haucer."

"I do hope that you're going to tell me that they're still working their shifts," Riorik asked, a tinge of hope in his voice.

"Hob, what part of '*I'm drowning in work*' made you think that any of us have gotten to go home in days? Fisk. I'm all-but living outta my office."

"An unfortunate way to live, to be sure," he conceded. "Any idea of what's been giving the Holy General cause to send so many ships into our humble abode?"

"Hah. Figured you'd already know by now."

"Knowing, and hearing what is already known repeated from a trusted source are two different things entirely," the Hobbler replied. "It helps to cut to the quick."

Mel stood up and leaned her head out the window while she answered him. "Well, then, even though you *must* already know it all, word is that she's gearing up for a new Imperium War. Got everyone on edge. So, she's demanding all the *sylverine* she can get."

"Yes. It's been going out by the cartload from the main gate."

She ducked back inside and blinked at him, the crease in her forehead deepening as she suddenly looked absolutely bewildered. "What idiot do you have on payroll over there?"

That was far from the response he expected. "Pardon?"

"Did I stutter? What idiot do you have over there that's not been payin' attention?"

Riorik's eyes narrowed and he shifted his stance slightly, straining his shoulders and sucking in his gut. "Explain, my dear, please."

Utterly oblivious, the private put his foot in his mouth without bothering to think. "Do we have time for this?"

The Hobbler was happy to help him remove it. "We're making the time. Badin is more than capable of delaying the *Hullbreaker* from departing our fine home. Mel?"

"What's going outta the gate is just trash. Barely more than fist-sized chunks. The real stuff? It's being shipped out under the guise of private merchants. The *Ladine* down there? Oh, she's marked as a Blackstone-owned hauler, but reality? Has more of the Queen's merry maiden-fiskers on it than the *Hullbreaker* ever will."

Galagrin looked out the window towards the ship she had just gestured at, then stepped outside her office for a better look as Riorik digested this bit of information. "This is... intriguing. How has it been kept secret for so long? It is beyond me that this hasn't made it in my direction."

"Fisk if I know," she answered with a shrug. "Been going on for months now. Though I am gonna say that they've been keeping their lips tight on the whole mess. I mean, guess I can say that the only reason *I* know is because I keep track of the records and all that shit. Figured it out myself just a handful of weeks back."

"Hm. Now I wonder why I haven't heard a peep about this. I knew about the pressure she's placed on the mines and the why, of course. You would think she'd be in less of a hurry to start a fresh round of pain with the Empire with all the trouble going on in the west with the League."

Mel looked at him and sighed. "Do I look like a tactician? You know as well as I do that the second cultists of Neph pop up, everyone gets all antsy and angry."

"Yeah, there've been a lot of uncomfortable things that have trickled down through the 13th Garrison and other places," Galagrin replied from outside. "I can attest to that. Listen though, that's why we're here."

"Thought you were here because of an attempt on one of the Queen's leaky rafts?"

"The poison was made *by* one of those cultists..." he clarified.

All the color left her face as her eyes went wide. "You're... kidding."

"Wish we were m'am. I found it earlier today. About exhausted now, if I can tell you the truth."

The Hobbler looked out at the door at him and for a moment, felt pity for the sag in his shoulders and the way he favored his stomach each time he moved. "It's true. The boy found the sad little lair that was being used by one of the Circle's own. My men found the cultist himself. He was quite vocal when I put my mind to him."

"Surprised that we didn't hear him screaming all the way down here if you decided to work him over."

"My my. Are you suggesting that I have a way with people?"

"Nope. I'm flat out accusin' you of it."

Galagrin cleared his throat and popped back into Mel's office. "Boss Hobbler? Boss Mel? Not to interrupt, but I... I think I have an idea. I don't think I like it."

"Oh? Do tell," Riorik said with a cross between irritation and amusement creeping into his voice. "I am sure the insights of a soldier barely out of the womb are worth hearing."

"Aw, now be nice to him Hob. Boy's got a job to do like the rest of us."

He took a deep breath and explained himself before the Master of Thieves could comment further. "This guy we're hunting, Ralafon? You said he's some kind of spymaster for the Civans?"

"That he is. He was promoted after the refugees started to flood the city. Think he was from that accursed little stain on the mountains all this headache has come from."

Galagrin looked out the window at a small ruckus going on near the *Hullbreaker* while Badin continued a screaming argument with her captain. "You two don't exactly get along, right?"

"I tolerate his existence," Riorik replied. "I have been quite careful that what he gets out of the city is limited to what I want him to. What I find out about what he knows is... passed on... to those with enough knowledge to make best of it. Really it's a bit pointless; there's very little that comes through here that is worth reporting about. I get paid quite well for it."

"Maybe *you* don't know about this because *he* knows about this, and maybe he's getting things past you that you don't know about."

The Hobbler's gaze suddenly went ice cold and the look on his face made Galagrin feel like he was little more than a bug on the floor. "Pick your words carefully. Are you implying that he has somehow subverted my operations?"

"If he did, then you think he'd waste time going after the *Hullbreaker?*" he slowly, softly asked. "Sounds like the real prize is the *Ladine* if it's loaded with ore. Would make more sense to want to see it hampered than some random *Legata.*"

Mel looked back and forth at the two men as realization dawned on her face. "If the Civan knows about it..."

"It would mean...," Riorik started, "Shit. Private, that is both brilliant and unsettling. There is a bright future ahead of you if you continue to use your brain. Never stop. Mel...?"

She turned away and shot out of her chair, shoving half of her body out her window. **"KELCHEN! WHERE IN THE PIT ARE WALLGON AND HAUCER!?"**

A quick shout of "Comin' boss! They're comin'!" answered her.

"IF THEY AIN'T HERE IN THE NEXT THREE MINUTES, YOU'RE SUCKING BILGE OUTTA -"

Kelchin almost barged through her office door with two exhausted, dirty men behind him. "Here! They're here!"

The first of the two to greet them had bleary, weary eyes hidden behind a mass of barely-blonde hair that covered his forehead, and a ragged beard that hid his mouth and most of his neck. "Boss Mel, we're here, what can I..." he began before he saw the other person in the room and bowed his head. "Boss Hobbler. Didn't hear you were -"

"Doesn't matter what you've heard," he testily retorted. "I'm here now, and you need to answer a question. Quickly, and honestly."

Hauser dropped his head right after Wallgon did and didn't meet anyone's eyes. "Boss Mel, Boss Hobbler. Anythin' you need. What can we do?"

All Riorik had to do was to gesture at Galagrin and the sword on his hip to get him to draw it out again. "Did *either* of you accept a bribe today from a stout-looking man? Silvery hair that goes to his shoulders? Looks younger than he is?"

"From a guy that looks like that? Nope, not at all," Wallgon quickly replied.

Mel didn't quite buy it. "Did you accept *any* kinda bribe, Wallgon? *Any* bribe from *anyone?*"

"Today? No, not today."

"If you're lying to me, you're in so much shit. You understand that, right?"

Looking around her crowded office, he just shrugged. "You, Boss Hobbler, and the army are all here, and you're asking questions? Boss Mel, I got a feeling that if I lied, I'd not live long enough to suck bilge."

"You're not wrong," Galagrin chimed in.

Wallgon swallowed nervously and took a deep breath. "Now I'll admit that there've been times where somethin' special has gotten placed on one ship or another after a couple of coin have dropped in my pockets, but you know I've always been honest about payin' my tithe to you."

"I would trust you've been honest about paying your tithe to *me* as well," Riorik said – not so much asking a question as he was clarifying his answer.

"Absolutely, Boss Hobbler. I don't want no trouble with either of you. I need this job. I like it here. If I had taken a bit of pay on the side today, I'd tell you. Last one I got was last week, and that was to..." he stopped and looked over at Galagrin. "Bosses? Do I gotta say? I mean, he's..."

Both Mel and Riorik answered at the same time. "Yes."

The private shrugged his shoulders and placed his left hand under the flat of his sword. "Don't look at me. I don't think I'm here as a soldier. I'm more of an... um..."

"The private is a... consultant," his 'new friend' replied. "It is safe to say that he is picking which topics and to whom he consults on very carefully."

He nodded vehemently. "Very."

You could tell that Wallgon didn't believe it to hear it, but he had the wherewithal, at least, to recognize that he didn't have a choice. "Then ah, it was from Dalin Havnil. Had a girl he wanted to disappear. Girl was as full of a kid as she could be. Guess his wife didn't want her around."

"Ah, just to make sure I understand – so I don't consult the wrong way – you helped smuggle her out of the city, right?" Galagrin quickly asked. "Not something else?"

"I'd not 'something else' a pregnant woman. I got standards!"

"I hope you do, because Mel is going to make sure you didn't,"

Riorik warned. "Won't you?"

"Can promise you that, Hob. Smuggling is one thing, but *something else-ing* a pregnant woman? That's another." She raked her eyes over at the shifting, sweating, bald man standing right against the doorway. "Haucer. What about you?"

"I uh... I don't want to get in any trouble..."

Riorik wrapped his hands around the club dangling off of his belt. "Then answer quickly."

The dockworker's eyes went wider, if such a thing was possible. "I... I did? He just wanted me to put some... you know. On the ship."

"Some *what*, Haucer?" Mel pushed.

He pulled out a bag from the inside of his tunic and dropped it on the floor. A little bit of yellow gunk dripped out onto the boards as he tried to back away from it. "Wasn't... wasn't hard to get on the ship. Said to put it on the *sylverine*."

"On the ore?" Riorik asked. "Did he say *why* to put it on the ore?"

"I asked that too. Said it wouldn't do much, just ruin the batch in refinement," he replied. "All he said. Paid... paid a lot. Was gonna turn it in end of shift, pay you both, swear I was gonna..."

Galagrin looked down at the bag on the floor, then stepped close enough to poke it with his sword. "I don't know so much about these kinda things, but um? Bosses? Doesn't *sylverine* do things to magic?"

"It magnifies the effects of it," Riorik said, drumming his fingers on the end of his club.

"Boss Hobbler, I got a feeling that pouring demon blood on something that makes magic stronger isn't gonna go well for anyone that picks it up after."

Frowning, his companion stared down at the pouch. "Oh I am long past the point where I can claim to understand some of the minutiae over how what works with what. Yet, I sense you are quite right, and it's obvious that Ralafon knows. Or thinks he knows."

"Which ship, Haucer?" the harbormistress asked. "The *Ladine?*"

He shook his head and pointed at another ship floating down the river. "The *Ladine?* Naw boss, not that one. The *Orboria.* She got hung up by an inspector. She just pulled anchor not more than five minutes ago."

"The *Orboria* isn't a cargo ship. She's a courier vessel," Mel said as her voice trailed off to a groan. "Oh, shit. Riorik? How dangerous do you think this substance is?"

"It comes from demons and they're fighting a small war with the things up north," Galagrin answered before the other man could answer. "Considerin' the firepower that's being brought to bear on the stuff up there, I'm gonna say that it's a lot. "

She looked down at her ledger and turned two pages before unleashing a plethora of profanity that managed to even make the Hobbler take a step back. "**KEL! GET CANNONS ON THE ORBORIA!**"

He ran up to her window, eyes huge. "Cannons? She isn't capable of carrying any and she's already set sail so I don't know -"

"Don't put them on her, SINK HER!" she shouted.

Riorik frowned and tried to belay her order. "That's a bit rash. We can simply have someone yell at her to stop, can't we?"

"If that poison as bad as you think, *and* it's made from demon blood and it's gone on metal that amplifies magic?" she said as she picked up her ledger. "Means it's gonna make whatever that blood does worse?"

"Yes? I thought we covered that in the case of our urgency, but it seems that you're overreacting."

Mel pointed at a line in the books and tried to hold back another flabbergasted shout. "Her next stop is the *capitol!* She's due to take a sample of the local mine off to the Chief Metallurgist!" She tossed it to her desk and grabbed his tunic with one hand while pointing at the *Orboria* with the other. "If it gets there, Gods only know what'll happen!"

"Oh shit," Galagrin quietly groaned.

"You may not be overacting, but I'm not inclined to see what it carries go into the water," the Hobbler mused. "It may make matters even worse."

"Then what the fisk do you suggest we do about it?" Mel charged. "I can't promise I've got anyone that can catch up to it in open water. It's the fastest ship that's in along the coast right now, bar none!"

It only took a minute to come up with the idea, though it wasn't much better than the one Boss Mel had. "Galagrin? Go fetch Badin. See if he can't think of a way to stop it without sending it to the bottom of the river, my good man."

As far as he was concerned, that was the best idea that anyone had come up with so far. He answered with a quick "Yessir," before running out the door with Kelchin right behind him. While Melaine's lackey shouted for help to try and get the *Orboria's* attention, Galagrin's shouts reached the battlemage's ears first.

Finally giving up on his attempt to talk sense into Captain Taes, hearing his friend's strangled cries was music to his ears. "Stop the ship?

What?"

"DO IT NOW! THINK OF SOMETHING JUST GET THEM TO STOP!"

Badin stopped there for a moment, looked downriver, and gave a little shrug. "Hm. Well, if that's what they want..."

Boss Mel and Riorik stepped out of her office and watched him run down the river as the ship started to slow down. "I suppose it's gonna be too much to ask that the guard doesn't come down here and swarm my docks, isn't it."

"I'm afraid it may be out of our hands; I am under no doubts that the shadows of Gonta are about to have some light cast into them. *Hopefully* I'll be able to bribe my way out most of it. For what it's worth, Aloric isn't happy about this either."

Hauser overheard him and made a strangled little cry. "The... the Overseer? I didn't know, swear I didn't know nothin' about..."

"A statement I'd make sure everyone believes, were I you," Riorik warned. He sighed and briefly looked at the handful of soldiers running up to Mel's office, only to be stopped by the well-meaning private Galagrin. "I do hope that the battlemage doesn't do *too* much damage. I realize by his nature that people are going to notice whatever he does but if he can be *somewhat* discrete, it would -"

Down on the riverbanks, Badin sized up the *Orboria* and the distance between them. After taking a minute to consider his options, he pulled his sword out of its sheath and planted the tip of it just past the edge of the water. He closed his eyes and whispered, "*Seaspark*," before opening them and shouting it out a second time loud enough to boom out over the harbor.

"*SEASPARK!*"

A crackling streak of electricity coalesced in the air around his head in a halo before discharging into his shoulders and down his blade. A trio of bolts arced out of his sword and illuminated the river before jumping out of the water and connecting against the mast of the *Orboria* in three different places.

Thunder rolled over the harbor as the sails caught fire and wood shattered. Badin gave a happy cheer as the boom went one direction and the rest of the mast went the other. Mel watched it unfold with her jaw hanging open. Riorik simply sagged back against the wall of her office. "Hm. You were saying, Hob?"

After a few quiet moments from the thief, he finally replied to her. "I strongly sense that Aloric is not going to be happy about this. Nor, I imagine, the Eastern Float-Commander."

"Hey, at least it's not like you're the head of a criminal enterprise that they could throw in the dungeon if they really wanted to crack down on the people that work at the docks," she said with a bit of a smirk. "You know, if they work their way up the chain."

"My, my, Mel. Is that your way of saying that you'd not be going to the gallows alone?"

"Oh, that's a given. You positive that this was worth it?"

He sighed as the mast sunk into the river. *Unexpectedly,* however, were the arrows and crossbow bolts that were suddenly launched of her deck at the no-longer-cheering battlemage on the riverbank. It spoke loudly for his character that instead of retaliating, he simply settled on ducking and trying to find cover.

When a fireball the size of Riorik's stomach lazily spun off of the ship at him, Badin broke out in a terrified run. "Oh, shit," she muttered. A second fireball was only stopped from hitting his face by a hastily flung bolt of lightning that intercepted and blasted it apart.

"That's more firepower than I would have given that ship credit for," the Hobbler awed.

Mel cleared her throat and cringed. "Prolly also should've maybe mentioned that there's a couple of Hunters and a battlemage of their own on-board that one, serving as an escort."

Riorik winced right along with her. "Oh. Dear, yes, I suddenly feel quite bad about it. I can't see him so well; how's he faring?"

"Not bad, really," she said as he managed to lunge under part of the docks and narrowly miss another fireball that detonated a huge chunk of river-rocks and mud.

"I suppose if ours makes it back safely we should reward him somehow, given what he seems to be going through."

Mel looked out of the corner of her eye at him. "Before or after the Queen has him hung for blowing up one of her ships?"

"That would depend. He's not trying to sink it, is he?"

"No, though I don't think he could now if he wanted to. Some men just poured off of another ship down there and... oh." Two guards charged under the wharf after him and he scrambled out the other side, hands up and trying to shout at them that he was with them and that he had to do it.

They didn't believe him, and he went down hard – with one of his teeth flying in the other direction – when one of the guards caught him with a haymaker punch right on his chin. "Oh?"

"Don't look like he's gonna get the chance even if he wants to."

"Would likely do him more good if we rewarded him now instead of later then, I think."

"Or call a medic for him," she added. "Maybe two."

On the deck of the *Hullbreaker*, her captain was having an entirely different conversation with the crew. "Alright everyone! Prepare to pull anchor. It's time we were on our way."

His helmsman nodded crisply and went for the ship's wheel. "I'll get us as close to the *Orboria* as I can."

"No, you won't."

"But sir...?"

Taes walked over and pushed the sailor away from the wheel. "We are on a tight schedule, Midshipman, and we're already behind. I'm in no mood to deal with any more of this madness. Put a handful of archers on him, and if he appears that he's getting loose from the men holding him down, leave him full of holes."

The sailor looked perplexed, but backed away per instructions. "Ah, yes sir. Any other orders, Captain?"

"Yes. Bring me flagon of something to drink. Yelling at that fool dried my throat out a bit and I don't feel like wheezing with every breath on our trip."

"Right away, Captain. I'll tap a keg below-deck."

"No, not from one of those," he testily snapped. "Bring it out of my personal stores. I'll only be drinking from it while we're on this patrol this tour."

The sailor paused and tilted his head. "Sir? May I ask why, sir?"

Taes smugly smiled at his subordinate. "I bought something special this time. Treating myself."

"If anyone deserves it sir, it's you. Consider it done."

After the helmsman darted out of sight, the Captain reached into his leggings and rubbed some coins together. *Don't get what all the fuss is about; had a sip of the stuff myself. Didn't do a damn thing but make my tongue numb for a moment. Just a little something in the drink to make us a little late to our next port of call without arousing suspicion. Not the first time a smuggler has needed a window opened by the navy, won't be the last.*

The Captain would have a long trip to find out if he was right.

V. MUDBATH

There was a lot to be said for the morning after you nearly sink a royal courier ship, stopped a mass poisoning, and helped arrange for one of the Plaguelord's cultists to show up in front of the local Temple. Most of the things you could say were *bad*, but there were a lot of them you could say. "Good morning, specialist," Galagrin called out from the barrack's courtyard.

That was not one of them. "It is *not* a good one," Badin grumbled.

The private looked up from the bag of gear he was securing to his horse. Technically, it wasn't *his* horse, but the one that Akaran had left behind when he took a magic-enhanced shortcut back up the mountains. "Doesn't feel like they are anymore."

"And you've only been involved with this for how long?"

"Less than a week. Barely got to Toniki before they sent me down here with that exorcist."

Badin shook his head in resignation. "Been meaning to ask. What's your read on him? Decent man?"

"Why?"

"Well, if I'm going up there, I'd like to know what I'm walking into."

"What, and get your surprise spoiled?" Galagrin quipped. "Naw, if you insist on coming, I'll tell you the honest truth: I've never met one before, and I don't think I want to again. Still, he's worth following, I think. Still pissed at myself that I missed the big fight."

The battlemage frowned and took a guess. "The one at the Row?"

"Yeap. He had me off scouring merchants for this and that. Stuff he needed for spells. If I'd been there, might've been able to help."

Badin grabbed the sack and helped him adjust it. "Or might've gotten dead and missed all... this."

"Oh, yeah. Because digging out in the dump was *so* much fun."

"Does it smell as bad up there?"

"Too cold to smell much of anything. How's your jaw?"

He ran a gloved hand along his cheek and winced. "I got an apology from the patrol on the docks. Honestly can't say I blame them; I'd have hit me too. Did you hear about the captain of the Orboria?"

Hefting the horrifically-foul-smelling sack up onto Nayli's back, he sighed with his reply. "No, what?"

"They had to quarantine her," he replied as a pair of maids walked past them and made a retching sound as the odor hit. "She went below-deck to check on the ship, fell, got a face-full of that shit the cultist was using."

"Ugh. Pits. She gonna be okay?"

Badin watched them go and earned a nasty look when one of them realized he was staring lecherously at her ass. "I hope. Inniat was tending to her when I was taken to the temple. Guard Command wanted me to get the 'best of care,' for 'service to the Queen.' Nice a reward as any for blowing up a courier ship."

Galagrin finished tying the sack down and grinned a little. "Always could be worse, suppose. Least it was just a few punches, not the gallows."

"Truth there," he agreed. "Oh. Inniat. Said to tell you he was proud of you. That you did good. Think he might have taken a small shine to you."

"No offense to the man, but he's not my kinda folk. Too stuck in the thinking of a matter, less the doing."

"More truth. His kind is always about 'what to say,' 'how to say it,' 'don't drink on duty,' 'mind your manners,' 'be respectful,' and all that shit."

That earned a hearty laugh from the younger soldier. "You'd think men like him would know that this *is* us minding our manners."

"You would," Badin shot back. "Well, my bags are packed. You sure you gotta take that foul smelling *thing* up to the village?"

"Sure it's gonna make me wanna be sick."

"Well, as long as you're sure of it."

Galagrin looked around the courtyard and climbed up on the horse. "Can I admit that I'm a little surprised that the Adjunct isn't here to see us off?"

"Inniat's got his hands full. Whole Temple is pissed. Be glad we're leaving."

"Oh? Why?"

The battlemage slung his rucksack over his shoulders. "This is a mix of what Inniat said when he visited me, and what I heard while I was being treated, so this ain't entirely official just yet."

"All that means is that we aren't supposed to bust some heads for another couple of hours."

Badin smirked. "You got that part right. Inniat has put in a formal request for an 'anti-corruption investigation' to be carried out between the city garrison, the army, the navy, and the temple. Word is he's got a very detailed list of places to look into, though for *some* reason, there's a few places on the east side that aren't to be touched, and he seems to think that the harbor has already been scoured."

"Oh, piss," the private groaned. "Well, I'm betting Riorik and Boss Mel are happy about that. But... oh, *piss*."

"Somewhat, I'd assume. As far as the piss?" he asked. "You got it. We don't want to be anywhere near this. I overheard him talking to some other priest, guess he had scribes go raid Pegilo's den."

"That couldn't have gone well."

He shook his head. "Not even close to well. They found some more journals, bunch of other stuff. I didn't ask what, but he said they'd have to compile all of it... for the Order of *Love*. Can you imagine how much he hated to say *that?*"

Galagrin tried to choke back a horrified laugh. "The Order of Light, asking the *Harlot's* people to help? I bet he's furious."

"Oh, he started cursing right after saying that. Shocked everyone."

"Piss," the private half-laughed, half-groaned. "Maybe we can't leave."

Badin cocked his head to the side as they started to walk away. "Eh?"

"Akaran, the exorcist? He's one of Hers."

"*Piss*. I thought people were just blowing smoke? Some *Oo-lo* maniac is leading the investigation in Toniki?"

"He's not that bad, really," Galagrin replied. "Don't think you're wrong about the maniac part. Nice enough guy, but there's an edge to him. I don't wanna be on the wrong side of him. So if Inniat has information..."

"If he's got it, he's not sharing it yet," Badin said, scratching at his chin. "Got the vibe that he's planning on turning over a bunch of rocks and see what he can drag out."

"That could take an hour."

"Or a week," the battlemage cautioned. "He said he was making sure he 'purged the corruption' that cultist was steeped in. Whatever that means, I don't want any part of it so, private, think it's best we get going. He gave me two copies of his request to make sure that the exorcist comes back down here when he's finished in Toniki."

"Two?"

"Just in case something happens to one of us. Guess he really wants the message delivered."

"Go here, go there, kill this, bury that, carry a corpse, carry a letter."

"Blow up a ship," Badin added.

The private didn't even bother to hide the laugh. "Blow up a ship. That was fun as all to watch, you know that, right?"

He flashed an ear-to-ear grin up at him. "More fun to do it. Think I'll get to bring down some lightning up there?"

"Not a question of *if*," he warned. "Question of *how much*."

Inniat left Gonta the same morning for a trip up the mountains, but in an entirely different direction with an entirely different purpose. It had taken a day of unpleasant hiking and horseback riding to get to their destination. Credit had to be given where it was due; the fact that his unwilling guide was even able to find the cave was impressive.

Of course, he had motivation.

Motivation brought on by the unceasing (and often repetitive) questions from the Lower Adjunct. Nobody – not the two scribes that traveled with him, nor the four local guardsmen – could tell if Pegilo was suffering as much as they were from the constant stream of interrogatories. If he wasn't, it was only because he was already mad. When they finally did reach the cave entrance, Inniat's questions shifted from the routine of 'Who are you working with' and 'How many of them are there' to something more pointed.

"So then. As I am to understand: *you* were the one to find the foci for the demon that attacked our city, the same one that brought those *shiriak* along with it? And you found it here?"

Pegilo shook his head rapidly from side to side and struggled against the chains that held his hands tight behind his back. "Didn't find, no, not here. Found it, not here."

The Lower Adjunct looked down at the journal one of his scribes was carrying, and stared in stone silence until the priest-in-training quickly turned the pages. "Ah. Yes. One page full of dim-witted scrawlings accompanied by matching drool stains looks much like the other. Thank you, Azala."

"Yes sir, you're welcome, sir," the wine-haired teenager nearly gushed in response.

He ignored her over-zealousness and frowned as he read over the cultists' ramblings. "*This* horrific little shithole is where you... what is it, exactly?"

"This is where he discovered plans to spread a plague throughout Gonta," the scribe clarified.

"Yes, Azala. I *am* capable of reading," he scolded. "The point of this exercise is to get this fool to admit it from his own mouth."

Her shoulders dropped as their prisoner answered him. "Through Gonta? To spread growth through the kingdom. That was the deal. That was the arrangement."

"This is the part that I had the most trouble understanding. Please do illuminate us."

Pegilo groaned in either pain or frustration – it was hard to tell which at this point. Nobody had seen fit to give him anything more than worn-out sandals for shoes, and the reason his hands were clasped behind his back was because Riorik had done such a job on them that there was no way to get his arms going back to the front without a great deal of effort from the city healers.

Effort that nobody had wanted to give. "The dealmaker! He offered growth to Growth in exchange for growth!"

"That's about how he phrased it in his journal, too," the scribe confirmed. "Although what it means..."

Inniat nodded at one of the guards flanking him. Without even asking what he wanted, the soldier pulled a dagger out of his belt and pressed the tip cruelly into Pegilo's shoulder. While he screamed, the Adjunct spoke directly to the soldier. "What was it you said your name was, again?"

He pulled his helmet off and glared at the priest. "Austilin. We've met."

"Ah, yes. We have. Rainstorm, wasn't it?"

"It poured."

"I imagine the guard is grateful that you recently signed up."

The thug (hired or otherwise) gave a seeping glare to everyone present. "Signed up? I've been in the guard since I was thirteen."

Nobody thought to challenge him. If he said he'd been in the guard for thirteen years, he'd been in the guard for thirteen years. "Ah… oh. Now, Pegilo, answer again. What exactly did you do here? Answer as if what's left of your life depends on it."

He whimpered, but quickly complied when Austilin's knife pressed against his swollen shoulder again. "The owner of the hand! He made the deal to spread growth!"

"The owner of the hand? The demon?"

"The owner the hand had! The man before the ungrowing soul! Before he was the ungrowing soul!"

Inniat's eyes narrowed slightly as he leaned forward on his horse. "Are you saying that the demon was a man before he… was a demon? Such a thing isn't possible."

The cultist shook his head and tried to fight his restraints once again. "We grow! We all grow! And here — look, here, this is what he did!" He struggled against the binds even harder and worked himself free of Austilin's grip as he gestured wildly into the cave with his head. "Follow, please, follow and you'll see!"

Inniat slowly dismounted and stood beside his horse as he picked his next words carefully. "It bears repeating, I think, that these ravings are not to be expressed or repeated. It would not set well in the minds of the average peasant that a madman postulates that you can become a demon of some power once you die."

The scribe nodded her head in agreement. "I can think of many of the unscrupulous that would try to find a way to empower themselves after death…"

"Yes, quite. That is *not* something the Gods would stand for, thus, it simply cannot be true. Were it so, I have no doubt that there are those who are desperate enough whom would let the idea guide them into violent delights seeking to gain the favor of the underworld."

"If demonhood smells like that yellow-skinned pukepot, count me out," Austilin grumbled.

"*However,* scribe, make sure you record everything you see here. Leave no detail out. The rest of you? Understand that we will all have to testify before the Priestess to this, and potentially the Provincial Maiden."

"You said that on the way up," he grunted again.

Inniat spared him a glare as he lead the way into the cave, a ball of white light sliding down the sleeve of his tunic to illuminate the passageway. "It bears repeating."

Several long minutes later, most of the party was deep

underground. Two of the soldiers had stayed outside to watch the entrance, but the rest of them were confronted by a rank pool of bubbling tar with a hint of rotten eggs thrown in for good measure. The cultist carelessly charged through the muck and nearly tripped into it at one point before Azala caught him.

He dropped down to his knees next to a piece of blackened wood halfway buried in the muck. "This, here, this. This is the way growth was to grow!"

The Lower Adjunct made his way over and pulled it out of the sludge with an involuntary shudder. After a few moments of reading, he frowned and looked over at his escort. "This is bizarre. Barely legible, and bizarre. I... I hear it more than I see it..."

"The dealmaker needed growth's touch," Pegilo ranted. "Needed a human that was young but growing to become one with the land, to stop growing as it was and to start growing as Growth does, to have her return to the true circle of life."

"In return, this 'dealmaker' would bring the 'touch of Growth' here after it bloomed in the girl's heart," Inniat added. "Correct?"

The cultist nodded vigorously. "Yes! You understand. But he couldn't. He didn't. *He* returned to the land, his body became one with the circle of life, but his *soul* did not go to Growth as he had pledged it would! It was taken from Growth, frozen! Growth couldn't grow in his soul! It was stopped, he was turned to ice!"

"This dealmaker. You mean he died and... he was denied to your master. Someone else made him a frozen monster."

Beside him, the scribe stared down at the wood and couldn't make any sense of the barely-legible scribbles. "To be clear, when you say 'Growth,' you do not mean Kora'thi."

"The Pretender?" he scoffed. "The one that takes credit for growth that She did not originate? No! I speak of true Growth!"

Austilin stepped right to the edge of the pond and tried to hold back a retching gag. The chamber couldn't have been more than seven yards across, and the pool of tar was easily three-fourths of that. "You're saying this dealmaker mulefisk made a deal with Neph'kor to... what, kill someone? And in return he was going to make a poison from her body and then try to infect us down here?"

"It does seem so. But he died before he could and the Plaguelord couldn't even claim his soul."

"He returned! But he returned, and not in service to our Lord! He is here, he is there, we search. What Growth was offered, what Growth *gave*, Growth *will* have, and *will* touch his heart with what it means to truly grow!"

"I don't know what that means, nor do I want to," the thug grunted.

Inniat nodded without looking at him. "With that, you and I are in agreement. So how did *you* come to all this?"

"The search for the frozen one brought me to here, where the deal was. Brought the two of us!"

That got everyone's attention. "Two of you? There's another one of your ilk here?"

"No, the other... Gumdin. Was... was a friend. Served Growth with me. When we found this place of growth, he was spoken to, and sent to search for the frozen one where it is cold," he answered, eyes going downcast as a touch of loss started to tremble in his voice. "I was given instructions to prepare the way and to help prepare this world for the growth that was agreed to!"

"Where is your friend now? What did you do?"

Pegilo looked up at him with a few tears in his eyes. Azala and the other scribe with her felt a pang of pity for him, however brief. "My friend he... I have not seen him since. He must still be in the mountains, growing. If he wasn't growing, then our Lord wouldn't have had need to send his tenders to search for him."

The Adjunct frowned again and tossed the rotten chunk of wood away from the pool of tar. "Tenders?"

"The tenders," he repeated. "They come from His home, and bear the scent of Growth upon their yellow flesh."

Once he realized he meant the *shiriak*, the last thing he wanted to do was remember the smell. "I see. Now, what did *you* do to prepare for this... growth?"

"Studied," he replied. "Waited. Watched. So little one like me could do until the tenders arrived at my door. Then the essence of the confused, cold growth. I found ways to aid them both. So few ways, it was only so soon that they appeared. So little I could do. But..."

"But? Faster, cultist, out with it."

"But I discovered a way to make growth spread! I did!"

Inniat stood up and backed away from the rambling madman and unsuccessfully tried to spit the taste of the air out of his mouth. "Then it's a good thing that you owned up to your sins."

"No sins. I never sinned. I did right by my Lord. I was loyal, loyal! More loyal than anyone!"

The Adjunct sighed and looked down at the contract carved into the wood. "No, I suppose you didn't. That much I think I can understand. It would be too much to ask or pray that you can shed some light on this man?"

Pegilo shook his head. "No, its a name. Not all names have meaning. Not all names have power. Sometimes a name is just a name for those that aren't supposed to know what a name is."

"All names have power, even ones we don't know," Inniat corrected. "I'm sure someone has to know who 'Sergibon' is. Though I cannot imagine there's many with the surname of 'Kalabranic' around these parts. Sounds like one you'd hear from somewhere closer to the Midlands than you would in Dawnfire proper."

"I do not know, I do not. Now... please? You promised you would let me see Growth, let me be growth?"

Inniat gestured over at Austilin, and he walked over without needing to hear what the priest wanted. "I did promise you that you would see Growth. I imagine She has words for you."

"She? My Lord is not a woman!"

"The Lords of all men are women," Azala quietly whispered. "Didn't you know? Even all of the Pantheon is guided by the touch of a Lady. Heard She's a bitch, too."

"Mind yourself, scribe. That almost sounds like you're giving respect to the Harlot," the Adjunct snapped.

"Of course, sir. I wouldn't dream of doing that," she murmured as a little something flashed in her eyes when he wasn't looking. "I doubt She would care so much about this matter anyways – this is a chore for men of Light, isn't it? Velveted hands and not gauntleted fists?"

Pegilo looked up at her and saw that flash a second time along with just a little hint of a smile at the corner of her mouth. "There is no matter! I gave as I promised I would give!"

"You get as you give," she replied icily. "Your master has given a little *too* much for Our taste. He should expect to be given some back – I imagine *you* will do well enough for a start."

Inniat looked over at his scribe and frowned. "Azala? Are you feeling quite alright? I've never heard you take a tone like that before... let alone interrupt me."

"Oh, no," she murmured again. "I... I apologize, Lower Adjunct. This just breaks my heart."

"Strange. I would have thought you'd be less passionate about this. You've always been so loving, and this is no work for a girl your age. I debated even bringing you along for unsettling you."

"That must be it then," she replied slowly and softly, a slight twinkle of light in her eyes. "I'm overwhelmed, that's all. It boggles my mind that someone so low would think that they weren't being watched or wouldn't be brought to judgment in due course. The Gods *do* see all and this mess has taken the *direct* attention of one or two."

"Hm. And now you speak of philosophy. No matter. Do mind your station and remember to not speak out of turn again."

He missed the haughty smirk that danced across her lips when he turned back around, though Pegilo didn't – although Austilin suddenly felt like he needed to reconsider his life's work.

"I'll do the best I can," she answered, then turning slightly to the thug-come-soldier, she mouthed, "You do."

Every ounce of color went out of his face.

Blind to the show behind him, Inniat turned his attention back to the cultist. "Now. Pegilo? The mandate of the Divine states quite clearly that your *misconception* of growth has no anchor in reality. Though, I must apologize. No growth will be had from your body."

"What? None? But how but you promised you -!"

Austilin threw a punch at the cultist and knocked him down onto his ass. Before he could try to recover, he drove his sword right through his hip and out the other side. "He promised you'd meet the Gods. Not how."

As Pegilo screamed, the thug-turned-soldier picked him up and tossed him into the rank muck. Inniat willed the ball of light hovering in front of him to grow brighter, and hotter, before dunking it into the sulfur and tar broth. "No growth from your body. Ash doesn't rot, and filth must be cleansed in light and fire."

The pond ignited.

Soon after, the cultist was cleansed.

Day turned into night, and the screams from the morning were matched by fresh screams at night. Long after the last of the sun's rays quit glistening on top of the river leading south from Gonta, a plethora erupted (although one of them was cut remorselessly short. The light from a burning boat, on the other hand, kept things illuminated as much as they needed to be. Sounds of owls and a few late-night frogs punctuated the last few gurgling moans coming out of the lacerated throat of the boat's captain, and served as a pleasant backdrop to Ralafon's cursing.

Two burly thugs had him by his wrists and forced on his knees in the reeds, and try all he could, there wasn't any hope of escape from them. The Hobbler stood a few feet away, desperately trying to scrub a glob of yellow gunk off of his coat. "Your family had best hope this washes out."

"Won't matter you fat prick, you'll be dead for this..."

Riorik sighed and gave up trying to get clean. "I am pretty certain that you were given a warning when we spoke last. You had a day to leave Gonta, wasn't that right?"

"Told you that you were a dead man, warned you that you were..."

"Yes, but you didn't actually do that, did you?" he charged. "You decided to stick around, give one more thumb into the eye of the Queen. You *know* I don't care about your petty squabbles with the kingdom, I simply care that you do it under *my* watch."

Ralafon looked up at him and tried to blink away the blood that was dripping into his eyes from a nasty cut on his forehead. "*Your* watch. You just care about... agh. About getting paid."

"I do," he replied. "That *is* why I care. Now that you've pulled this little stunt, my new friend in the priesthood is calling for an anti-corruption review. The army is inclined to agree, given that we had to de-mast one of the Queen's ships. That's going to cut into my profits tremendously."

"The least of your problems. The *least* of your problems."

Riorik sighed at the bluster and knelt down in front of him. "Oh? Care to educate me, astound me with whatever tale you have cooking up in your mind? One last exchange of ideas between business partners?"

"Weak. You're weak," he seethed. "The Queen is weak. Look around. All this military might, all of it just theater. Oh she throws gold at it. Throws gold around like it's water. Gold doesn't make an army."

"No, old friend, but it does buy them."

"Ask her how well buying loyalty works for her. This entire kingdom is gonna break," he taunted with a sneer. "Why do you think she has the royal bitch beat the drums of war every spring? Only way your Queen stays on the throne is when the fit and able are off getting killed."

The Hobbler had to nod at that. "While that much may be true, you forget the other side of having a military flux with money: they spend it. They keep themselves busy. They make men like me money, they make men like Aloric money, and they make friends with all the tradesmen – which makes me even *more* money. It's something that your Empress doesn't understand."

"My Empress rules through loyalty!" he shouted, crying out when one of the thugs twisted his left arm until something started to tear. "Not fear, not bribes. *Loyalty!* Something you don't understand and never will!"

"Loyalty, devotion, love, respect. All of those wonderful things. Yet mark my words, little spy: when push comes to shove, she will wish she had bought as many friends as she inspired. Friends that make each other money are the best friends, don't you know."

Ralafon looked up Riorik's face through his bloody tears. "Only thing I know, you fat prick, is that you're dead. You're gonna die painfully. You're dead. Your friends are dead. That *monster* that... that killed my preci... that killed Rmaci? The moment, the *heartbeat* he steps outta Dawnfire territory, he's gone. Word's out, Hobbler. Ain't gonna be any safe places for him past the border."

"I have this odd feeling that he may not live that long," he sighed, "but, I'll be sure to let him know. Would hate for him to walk into something blind and all that. Poor sod is just the kind of guy to end up having the deck stacked against him as it is."

The spymaster tried to laugh. Most of it came out as an anguished wheeze. "Won't matter. You won't live long enough to tell anyone. That shit on you... you don't know what it is, where it's from, it's -"

Riorik tried to wipe the stuff off of his coat again and sighed loud enough to interrupt him. "It's demon blood and corpse ash. I'm going to have to scrub for a *week* thanks to you. I'm going to have to show up at the temple, offer some piddling tithe to the priests, too. Probably get a lecture from that insufferable Adjunct while he finds a way to make sure the only taint left on my soul is my own now, damn unto all."

That was all it took to get Ralafon to stop struggling. "How did... how could you possibly know?"

"You idiot," the Hobbler snapped. "Because we found the moron you got it from. You think it was a fluke that we knew where to look on the docks? He told us where it came from. So help me, if I have to use up one of my favors with the exorcist because of you, I will come back and piss on your corpse a second time. How *did* you run across him, anyways?"

"What?"

"You're Civan. There's few groups that have a taste for followers of the Plaguelord, and the Order of Flame is assuredly not one of them," he pointed out. "Flame burns away rot, it purifies it. I am nothing like a religious man – even I can't muster enough dishonesty to claim otherwise – but I know that under the table, the Circle picks fights with

Illiyan followers every opportunity it gets."

Ralafon relaxed in their grip and rested his ass on his heels. "What of it?"

"Quite a lot of it," Riorik mused. "What possessed you to get into bed with him? I assume that you had some clue he was operating in the city, given your own nature, but... well, forgive me, but the timing is strangely suspect. He couldn't have been studying the demons for all that long; *something* would have leaked out if he had been after it for more than a few short weeks. One of my own men can attest to that. So. Why now?"

"What's in... what do I get for it? Free passage?"

He bellowed out a laugh that you could hear all the way to the city. "Oh I want to know, but I don't want to know that badly. No. This is a question of 'shorter death or longer one.' Or, maybe a question of a 'longer death and I don't start torturing others you care for in front of you as someone slowly disembowels you.' Your choice."

"You're not gonna kill me," Ralafon argued. "I'm too useful. I know people, have names, know things. You'd be leaving money on the table."

The Hobbler sighed at him and shook his head. "All this time together, and you fail to realize that there still are a few things that are more important than money. Putting an end to our relationship is, I must say, one of them." He shrugged and tried to straighten up his coat. "Again, it is your choice. I only offer this because of such good friends we have been in the past."

"Damn you."

"Too late for that, I am afraid. Though recent discoveries have changed my understanding of what it means to be faithful. I may have to reconsider my position on sin now because of it."

Ralafon coughed up a mouthful of blood and tried to spit on the master of thieves. "There's pain in your future, Hobbler. So much of it. Fine. You want to know how I knew about him?"

"Yes, though repeating my question back to me wasn't overly necessary. You're gaining nothing by trying to buy time."

"Was a woman. A trader."

"It's always a woman," he said as he rolled his eyes. "What was her name, what did she know? Oh, and how did she know it – if I can be that lucky."

He cried out as one of the thugs twisted his other arm almost to the point of no-return. "Anais. She had a companion, too. Scarred up motherfisker. He called her Lady Anais. Think... think I heard her call him Donta."

Riorik stood there and rocked back and forth for a moment before replying. "I... hmm. I think I have heard her name whispered around my territory before. A few years ago, nothing recent. She was here?"

"Yeah," he sighed. "About the time those soldiers got massacred up in Toniki."

"Interesting. I was never able to find out much about her. Calls herself a broker of information, yes?"

"Yeah. That's her."

"What did she offer, exactly?" he asked. "Remember, answer honestly. A lie is worse for you right now than an unpleasant truth. It's a long trip back home."

Ralafon cursed the men holding him and was rewarded for his insubordination by a fresh twist on both arms at the same time. "She... damn you. All she wanted was some information on some old relic. Last Empress had it. Lost it in one of the Imperium Wars. Urn of Xabraxis."

"I've never heard of it before. Tell me more."

"Don't know."

"Ralafon..."

The Civan quickly shook his head, new tears starting to roll down his cheeks. "I don't know! She said she knew someone that could help me get what I wanted. Just... needed to know if my agents had found the Urn!"

"And have they?"

"Might've. Just rumors. Some *Oo-lo* shrine or temple or whatever it is those fisking heathens pray at."

Riorik strummed his fingers on his side. "Rumors are diamonds in the right ears. Where is she now?"

"Don't know. Don't care. She told me about the rotten shit, I told her that it might be somewhere near Basion City. Don't know fisk else about it."

"Interesting. Very interesting. I'll have to look into the matter."

Ralafon looked over to where his compatriot had finally given up and finished bleeding out. "Now just... get it over with. Give me time to make peace with Illiya, then get it over with."

"About that," Riorik replied. He walked around his captive in a slow circle, pulling a hatchet out of his coat and shifting it back and forth between his hands. "Gonta is a decent walk away from here. What do you think, boys? About five hours by foot?"

The two thugs murmured in agreement.

"What? You said I'd get a quick death!"

"No, I said your choice was 'shorter' or 'longer.' You've earned 'shorter,' but it won't be 'quick.' Really, you usually pay much better attention to what people say."

Ralafon started to fight in their grip again, cursing each time a new muscle started to tear. "You... If you think you're getting me to walk back there you're out of your mind. Gonna make you work for it, every step of the way..."

"Oh, I know. I didn't think this was going to be easy. Will you indulge me one thing, before we begin the inexorable fight and battle of wills it's going to take to drag you back to Gonta?"

"I've done nothing but indulge you, you fat fisk!"

He couldn't see Riorik's smile, but the thugs did. Both of them wished that they hadn't. "I did promise that you'd be hanging from both of the city gates. So you will, and I just *know* that you're going to be stubborn about the whole thing. So before we start *that*, one small thing."

"Get it over with you windbag. Just... you're dead, I'm dead. We're all dead. Just dead men walking, you'll see."

"No, we're not."

"You plan to live forever? You really are delusional."

The Hobbler answered him with another hearty belly-laugh. "No, I mean... *walking*. Dead men, I'm sure, but *walking?* I feel as if there's one thing *everyone* has forgotten about me! All this fuss over who killed who, what plague is going to rip through the underbelly of the Kingdom, and it seems like everybody has had their eyes on a decaying hand. A hand! Hands are important, but..."

"But what?"

"But you're wrong. You can't be a dead man walking..." he started as the head of the axe glinted in the firelight, "if you don't have any *feet*."

End:
Saga of the Dead Men Walking: Slag Harbor

Did you enjoy your trip to the Harbor?
Don't forget to let me know how you felt about it! Your reviews, good or bad, help me figure out what to do better (or keep doing), provide social proof, and even let me advertise easier. Your feedback really helps keep

the pen filled with ink – and the computer filled with electricity.

Be sure to stop by the Amazon listing and drop your stars and your comments before you move on to the next book in the series...

https://www.amazon.com/dp/B07DX6MSPC

...because now it's time for a few of my Favorite Things.

Next:
Saga of the Dead Men Walking: Favorite Things

COMPENDIUM OF THE DAMNED, THE DIVINE, AND ALL THINGS IN-BETWEEN

13th Garrison / The 13th Ray of Dawn
The 13th is assigned to general peacekeeping operations throughout the Weschali Province. Stationed a day's ride away from Gonta, it is under the direct command of Commander Xandros Wodoria and his wife, the Battlemage Evalia Wodoria.

Abyss
The pit. The last stop for the damned. A place of darkness and flame; of madness and pain. The Abyss is overseen by the Great Dragon-God Gormith, otherwise known as The Warden. The Abyss is home for all of the Fallen Gods, who rule over their own regions – the individual Abyssal Canyons. Abyssians are creatures – be they damned souls twisted through eons of torture, or things born of the Abyss itself – that call the unholy realm home. Or at least, call it prison.

Agromah
A fallen continental-kingdom to the North of Civa, Dawnfire, and more, across the Nightmare Sea. It is believed by most that the armies of the Order of Love abandoned the Order of Flames in the face of a demonic army lead by Archduke Belizal and his son, Zeborak. It's this belief (false as it is) that lead to Niasmis being exiled from the Upper Pantheon, and her followers to suffer the Hardening.

Akaran DeHawk, Exorcist
A neophyte exorcist in the Order of Love. Holds several minor exorcisms under his belt before being dispatched to Toniki, including a full-blooded demon. Has an... interesting... past that he doesn't talk much about. Specifically, he doesn't remember most of it.

Arch-Adjunct Grimblebob
One of the eldest Adjuncts in the Temple of Light, he resides in the Dawnfire Capitol and has a hand in training other Adjuncts throughout the Kingdom.

Basion City
Located in the Kettering Provincial Region, Basion City is heralded as "The safest place in Dawnfire," due to being far from anywhere the Kingdom borders. It's home to a hospital, of sorts, for those exposed to unnatural rigors that have left the mind weary.

Battlemage
Soldiers (or mercenaries) trained in destructive magics. They do not do their work in service to their Gods (though a few combine their arts with worship), and they are not interested in scholarly pursuits (such as the mages of the Granalchi Academy). They use magic as a weapon, and by and large, are content to just do that.

Battlemage Evalia Wodoria
The wife of Commander Xandros Wodoria of the 13th Garrison. She's a battlemage, and a damn effective one at that. Don't get on her bad side, and for the sake of the Gods, DON'T let her hear you call her Xandros's pet!

Blackstone Trading Company (BeaST)
The largest trading company in the entire western hemisphere, the BeaST is owned and run by Master Aidenchal, a dedicated follower of Uoom, and it has holdings that stretch from Civa to Matheia and everywhere – literally everywhere – else.

(Former) Captain Orin
One day prior to the start of Slag Harbor, he was in charge of the Gonta Guard. However, after subsequently pissing off both Exorcist Akaran DeHawk and Battlemage Evalia Wodoria, he was relieved of his

command. He's lucky he wasn't relieved of his head.

Chief Metallurgist
The Chief Metallurgist is in charge of making sure that any and all ore mined anywhere in the Kingdom is refined to the standards of the Crown, if it's to be used by the Queen or her military.

(The) Circle
The twisted cult that adheres to the insane beliefs spouted by the God of Plague, Neph'kor. Much like their patron, they are universally hated and actively expunged whenever they turn up. Why anyone ever joins them to begin with is a matter that even the most concerned scholars have yet to figure out.

(The) Civan Empire
Located north of Dawnfire, and stretching across the entirety of the upper mainland and the coastline of the Cavisian Ocean. It is currently ruled by Empress Bimaria and honors the Goddess of Flame, Illiya, as its matron. It is in a rolling religious war with the Kingdom of Dawnfire – both for providing aid to the Goddess of Love, and a 'sisterly dispute' between Illiya and Melia, the Goddess of Destruction.

Coldstone
The Coldstone is a magical construct designed by the rogue Elementalist, Usaic, and hidden away in his tower north of the village of Toniki. The exact nature of it is relatively obscure, though it is coveted by at least one frozen monster, one conglomeration of damned spirits, an unceasing swarm of scavenger demons, an exorcist of the Order of Love, his mentor, a wisp from the Elemental Plane of Ice, and someone that calls himself the Man of the Red Death.

So whatever it is, it's powerful – and powerful objects always bring strife in their wake. The Coldstone is no different.

Dalin Havnil
A well-to-do merchant with ties to Maiden Piata. He thinks he can get away with anything, and frequently does.

Demons
Demons are powerful beasts that roam the pit. Most have some degree

*of sentience, but not all. It's a catch-all phrase for the pitborn. Daemons, on the other hand, are demons of **immense** power and ability. These creatures represent massive threats to the world of the living, and even the Mount of Heaven.*

Fleetfinger's Guild
The Guild of Thieves. While leadership structure varies from location to location, there is honor among them (contrary to popular misconceptions).

Fritan Guard
The unfortunate men and women that are tasked to uphold the laws of the Civan Empire at the Port City of Fritan, the last city of men on the cursed continent of Agromah. It's not what one would call a pleasant tour of duty. However, the Empress doesn't care who serves in it from what Kingdom, Empire, or League – so to some, it's considered a last-ditch place of employ, if you're desperate enough. The pay's pretty decent too, though there's never been a need for retirement funds.

Gonta (City of Mud)
The sub-capitol of Waschali Province. It's a three-day ride away from Toniki, and a day's ride from the 13th Garrison. The city is overseen by Merchant-Master Aloric Everstrand, Priestess of Stara Deboria Ult, and rumor has it, Riorik the Hobbler, Boss of the regional Fleetfinger's Guild.

Holy General Johasta Fire-eyes
A devout follower of Niasmis, Johasta is the military commander of the Kingdom of Dawnfire, and all of the Order of Love's paladins, exorcists, and templars answer to her as well.

(The) *Hullbreaker*
A Legata-class cruiser under the command of Captain Taes.

Imperium War(s)
The ongoing series of conflicts between the Kingdom of Dawnfire and the Civan Empire.

Justiciar
Judges in the Kingdom of Dawnfire. While larger cities have ones that are assigned to them directly, smaller villages have to rely on traveling

Justiciars to settle matters of legal dispute (or criminal proceedings of critical nature).

(The) *Ladine*
A cargo hauler under the flag of the Blackstone Trading Company, but due to its constant cargo of sylverine ore, it's guarded by soldiers under the command of the Queen's Navy.

Legata-class cruiser
The smallest class of the Queen's naval ships. They are capable of crewing up to fifty men manning oars, rigging, and the fourteen cannons (seven to a side) mounted on-board, as well as a single warballer.

Lower Adjunct
Priests of the Order of Stara that oversee the day-to-day operations of various Temples of Light. They answer to either the Temple Adjunct or the Priestess of Stara, depending on size and importance of the shrine in question. Due to the Order of the Purity's mission to defend the heavens, the vast majority of Lower Adjuncts attached to Temples of Light are Pristi followers.

Merchant-Master Aloric Everstrand, Blackstone's Marauder
Aloric is a mercenary-turned-merchant, and he has carried his warlike ways on the battlefield into the negotiating chambers. He is currently (and happily) installed as the overseer to the city of Gonta (though his reach spreads throughout much of the province).

(The) Missian League
A collection of city-states situated to the west of the Kingdom of Dawnfire. It has the unfortunate luck to be in the second-shortest distance between the Kingdom of Dawnfire and the Civan Empire. For reasons best relegated to the 'How can you be so stupid?' bin, the current Luminary that rules the League openly professes loyalty to the God of Plague. As a result, it's currently a battleground as Dawnfire is presently attempting to correct his misbegotten ways.

(The) Mount
The Heavenly Realms. Whereas the Abyss is the last stop for the damned, the Mount is the final reward for those that served the Gods or

lived an honorable life.

(The) *Orboria*
A courier ship in the Royal Navy, but it typically sails under the flag of the Blackstone Trading Company for the sake of secrecy and security. It should be noted that it says a lot that pirates are more threatened by ships that sail under BeaST colors than they are of ships of the Q.R.W.

Ogibus Bay
Ogibus Bay sits almost in the middle of the Alenic, and serves as a trading hub for merchants from Matheia, Sycio, Dawnfire, and the loosely-aligned island countries scattered throughout.

Order of Light
The Orders of Light are comprised of the various Gods and Goddess of the Mount of Heaven, with the exception of the Goddess of Love. The primary Order is the Order of the Pure, and Her followers typically direct the other Orders in all manner of interactions in the Kingdom of Dawnfire and beyond.

Order of Love (Oo-lo)
The followers of the Goddess of Love call the Order of Love home. It's divided into three separate branches: the Lovers, who spread the Word of Niasmis; the Templars, who use the boons of Love to heal the sick and injured; and the Paladins, the holy warriors and exorcists who use the powers granted by the Goddess to hunt and banish the dead and damned. The order of Love is perceived to be chaotic, as the nature of Love is often unpredictable, and the Order itself is the most aggressive of all of the Heavenly Orders in seeking to expulse the unholy from the world.

Despite being despised by most of the world, the Order of Love holds a special place in the Kingdom of Dawnfire, and has direct authority over the Grand Army of the Dawn. This authority has been granted by the Queen of Dawnfire herself, and as such, is incontestable (regardless of how much others may wish it so).

The phrase 'Oo-lo' is used as a slur to name the Temple or Her followers when in impolite company.

Order of the Pure
Followers of the Goddess of Purity. They protect the Temples of Light and will wage defensive battles (or at least, reactionary ones) against minions of the Abyss if they sense that the Heavens are under assault. Aside from that? A lot of people consider it a miracle if you see them do anything more involved than scratch their asses.

Overseer
The Overseer is a title for the local leader of a large village, township, or city – especially those that have been issued a Contract of Governance by the Queen, which allows an Overseer to be installed by one of the many Merchant Guilds throughout the Kingdom.

Pauper's Row
Situated on Gonta's west side, Pauper's Row sits along a canal filled with backwash from Rashio's Falls and the subsequent river named Ichaia's Tears. The poor, the hobbled, and the destitute huddle here. The Temple of Light in Gonta sits on a small hill that looks over the unwanted masses; a beacon for the lost.

Port Authority
The office that oversees all shipping coming in and out of port cities in Dawnfire. They also coordinate with the Navy's fleet commanders.

Priestess Deboria
The Priestess of Stara for the Temple of Light in Gonta. She has temporarily relocated to the village of Toniki to aid in defeating Makolichi, Daringol, and other unholy cretin.

Priestess of Stara
Separate from the individual priests and priestesses that serve the Gods of their respective Orders, a Priestess of Stara serves all the Gods by caring for the Shrines of the Order of Light and providing care for pilgrims or worshipers in need.

Privateer Wars
A series of bloody naval conflicts between several merchant guilds and pirate fleets in the Alenic Ocean. The wars continued until the Dawnfire Navy established control of a third of the Alenic, the Blackstone Trading

Company and the Admirals of Ogibus Bay each taking a quarter, and the Dunesires of Sycio the remainder.

Provincial Maiden
A Maiden is a title granted to a select few leaders in the Kingdom. Their words are law, and are often placed in charge of the Queen's primary interests, notably her armed forces. Most armies would call them "Generals" or "Admirals," but they are both more than that and less. Military-minded Maidens answer directly to the Holy General Johasta Fire-eyes, while other Maidens (few as they are) speak directly to the Queen herself. Each military Company is assigned and run by a Maiden as a matter of course.

Queen's Royal Wavecrasher (Q.R.W.)
Ships that belong to the Queen's Navy in Dawnfire.

Regulation One-six-three
A requirement in the Dawnfire Army Regulations stating that local guards/militias/other must provide shelter for any soldier of any rank that is passing through or is being temporarily stationed in any particular region.

Riorik the Hobbler
Boss Riorik is a portly man with deep pockets and few morals. He runs the Fleetfinger's Guild in Gonta and has contacts throughout the entirety of Weschali. Don't ask how he got his name. He might show you. And if he says you're his new best friend? You're probably wishing you weren't.

Sepulcher of the Lost
A graveyard for those too poor to have a proper burial.

Slag Harbor
A waste-dump located to the southwest of Gonta. A few days prior to Galagrin's adventure, Battlemage Evalia Wodoria encountered a Daringol wraith that had taken possession of a swamp beast. The results were not pleasant.

Sparkcaster Mage
Sparkcasters use the elemental power of electricity to power their spells.

As a result, most of their magic is used for offensive purposes (though occasionally as a component of Illusory spells).

Sycio
Complicated. In short, the deserts of Sycio were once ruled by the Dunesires and Duneprinces. As a culture, they had no problems consorting with the dead, the damned, and even had a strong workforce of corpses – a good body is a shame to waste. During the Age of Misfortune, one of those demonic alliances resulted in... why don't we say "aggressive discomfort" ...felt across all of the land.

Sylverine Ore
An oft-sought-out amber-colored metal that can be used to either temper steel to resist magics or to provide a base for magical enchantments to take hold (depending on your school of study and ability), sylverine ore is only found in two of Dawnfire's provinces, Weschali being one of them.

Temple (Shrine) of Light
The TOL is the generic name for any shrine, temple, or other structure identified as a house of worship for the Gods of the Pantheon as a whole. They are tended to by Temple Adjuncts and Lower Adjuncts, and the larger temples may be under the hand of a Priestess of Stara.

Toniki
A small village north of Gonta, and the northernmost town in the Kingdom of Dawnfire. Relatively unimportant, it boasted reasonable trade through both the efforts of the town alchemist, and the old Bolintop Mine. When the mine collapsed, trade slowed to a crawl.

At current, Toniki is currently under siege by the demon Makolichi, and the conglomeration of souls that named itself Daringol. Other entities (both good and evil) are involved as well; with the grand prize being a magical construct called the Coldstone...

Warballer
A ship-mounted siege weapon capable of launching thin metal balls filled with a variety of alchemetic compounds designed to neutralize opposing ships, port defenses, or ground-based soldiers. They can be filled with anything from explosives to toxic gasses (not that the Queen

would ever do such a thing), acids, or even reagents that react with magical attributes.

Weschali
The easternmost provincial region of the Kingdom of Dawnfire. It holds immense strategic value to the Kingdom, as the primary passageway through the Equalin Mountains between the Kingdom of Dawnfire and the Civan Empire. Among other villages and cities, it encompasses Anthor's Pass, Triefragur, Gonta, and Toniki. It is under the direct oversight of Maiden Piata and her Consort.

Defiled
The 'defiled' are mortal/natural creatures that have been exposed to or twisted by Abyssian magic/auras to the point that they have become monsters in their own right. Corpses that have arisen from the dead on their own volition are lumped into this category, as are animals (or even people) that have been corrupted past the point of the Laws of Normality. Creatures (and even inanimate objects) that have been turned pose as much of a threat to the living world as demons... and some demons have been known to start out this way.

The Defiled can also be considered a broad category for various breeds of creatures that can fit on either side of the 'formerly alive' and 'entirely demonic' spectrum. Wraiths, for example, are often simply the souls of the dearly departed; dogs and wolves, given the right nudging, can grow into Abyssian hounds.

At the Battles of Coldstone's Summit, the notable Defiled included:

Daringol
A conglomeration of damned souls operating as one entity. Daringol can spread its essence from person to person, corrupting their souls until their spirits become part of it – adding to the entity as a whole and possessing their bodies. For reasons unknown, it continually seeks out dead bodies as well, in a desperate attempt to find a 'home.' Currently hunted by Akaran DeHawk and his allies, so far, stomping it out and stopping the spread of its corruption has been neigh-impossible.

Makolichi

A demon originating straight from the Lower Elemental Plane of Ice, Frosel. It has been on a rampage through the mountains around Toniki for years, and a day prior to the events in Slag Harbor, attacked Pauper's Row in Gonta.

Shiriak

Vile, baby-like creatures that reek of sulfur and rot and bile and worse. These scavenger-demonkin are attracted to places of rot, decay, or mass slaughter. They can sniff out a massacre a hundred miles away, and can zero in on a plague just as easily. Servants of Neph'kor and His minions, they pose little threat.

Gods and Godlings

The World beyond the World is full of an infinite number of creatures and beings of immense power that dwarf anything mortal men can use. Some of those things are easier to cope with than others, and others still... are a different story entirely.

Illiya, the Goddess of Flame

Ruler of the Upper Elemental Plane of Fire, She has an ongoing rivalry with Her sister, Melia, the Goddess of Destruction. It should be noted that while Illiya is the Matron Goddess of Civa, Her sister is the Matron Goddess of Dawnfire. It is also worth noting that the followers of Illiya despise the Goddess Niasmis so strongly and fiercely that they persecute and kill anyone that bears allegiance to the Goddess of Love at any opportunity.

Niasmis (The Harlot)

Banished from Her rightful place next to the top of the Mount of Heaven by the other Gods and Goddess for an infraction against the Goddess of Flame that She truthfully did not do, the Goddess of Love is considered by nearly everyone to be the least of the Divine, and as such, holds power only in the lowest regions of the Heavens, and... well...
...She has a bit of a chip on Her shoulder because of it...

Neph'kor

God of Plague and Disease. Universally loathed and despised, even among the other Fallen. May well be the most hated Godling in all of creation. Despite that, He has followers everywhere – even if they're actively hunted by the priests of the Goddess of Purity, and openly challenged by the druids of Nature.

Makaral
The Berzerker God, the God of War.

(The) Neutral
Situated somewhere below the Pantheon but above the Fallen are Gods that are outside of the realm of Good and Evil. The Elemental Gods would fit in this category, were it not for the dual nature of all elements (life and death) that have earned them seats on the Pantheon and chains in the Canyons of the Pit. However, Uoom (the God of Death), Makaral (the God of War), and Eberenth (the Goddess of Knowledge), along with a scant few others – consider themselves neither aligned with the Heavens or the Abyss, and walk both sides of the next world relatively freely.

Their followers aren't necessarily shown the same permissions in the world beyond, but the Gods are.

Pantheon
The near-entirety of the Gods of Light. When one seeks to honor the Pantheon, they are honoring every God and Godling that aligns itself with the Mount of Heaven, and are honored (as a whole) at most Temples of Light. Not every Holy God is represented on the Pantheon, as some Elemental Gods do not seek such worship – and the Goddess of Love has had Her seat vacated as punishment for a perceived slight against the other members.

Pristi, the Goddess of Purity
As the name implies, Pristi is the Goddess of all that is pure, and serves as the Guardian of the Mount of Heaven and all souls that call it home.

THE MAGE'S HANDBOOK OF SPELLS, INVOCATIONS, AND OTHER FLASHY EFFECTS

Invocations

While Words get the point across, they're mostly just simple spells with relatively simple effects. The Order of Love is a unique outlier, too; most Orders don't use single Words as much as they do full-blown invocations. Niasmis's priests have been known to use longer, more convoluted requests for divine aid when the situation absolutely requires it, preferring instead to get the point across as quickly as possible.

Lumina, Lumina, cast shadows into nothing – cast all of your light into the dark!
This invocation, when called by a Priest of Purity, will generate a flash of pure light that will stun, burn, and briefly blind almost anything unholy caught within its radius.

Lumina, Lumina, show what shadows hide; show what casts them deep; show what blocks your light; show what swallows it whole.
This invocation, when called by a Priest of Purity, will expose any decay, Abyssian influence, illness, or physical injury on a person or in the environment within the radius of the spell.

Generic Spells/Invocations

Sometimes, you don't need to seek the favor of a God, or devote yourself to fancy spells and complicated abilities. And other times, the magic is either so rudimentary that anyone with so much as a sliver of affinity could cast the spell – albeit with the details slightly different from mage to mage and priest to priest.

Seaspark
A spell used by sparkcaster mages to send lightning traversing bodies of water before explosively reaching their destination. A seaspark can exponentially increase the distance a sparkcaster can send their electric currents.

Thundercall
A spell used by sparkcaster mages that conjures a bolt of lightning with various levels of intensity. You don't want to be on the receiving end of it, either way.

Wardmarks
Runic words written or etched onto an object that conveys a magical property or effect.

THE SAGA OF THE DEAD MEN WALKING

Year 512 of the Queen's Rule
The Snowflakes Trilogy
Book I: Snowflakes in Summer
Freshly minted by the Order of Love, a young exorcist is sent to the edge of the Kingdom of Dawnfire to deal with a 'small, simple haunting.' Between a winter that won't end, a girl that doesn't belong, and people being eaten in the woods, only one thing is for sure: he's over his head, and utterly out of luck.

Book II: Dead Men in Winter
As the search for the Coldstone continues, new allies enter the fray in the mountains around Toniki, and in the streets of the City of Mud. But new blood only means new bodies, and Makolichi seeks to provide those in excess...

Book III: Favorite Things
It's time for Usaic's Tower to ascend. Truths will be revealed, blood shall be spilled, and suffering shall become legendary. But it's not just the living who should fear the Coldstone being set loose. For though the dead will rise, the damned had best be ready for Who comes next...

Year 513 of the Queen's Rule
The Auramancer's Exorcism
Book I: Insanity's Respite
Beaten, broken, and battered, Akaran is sent to the Safest City in the Kingdom to recover from his battle against Makolichi, Daringol, Rmaci, and the rest. What he expects is peace and time to heal. What he finds instead is that insanity knows no bounds and offers no respite...

Book II: Insanity's Rapture
In life, the woman in his dreams had been a spy – a murderess, a liar, a fraud, and a thief. Sentenced to burn for her crimes, her screams have haunted his sleep since the moment she was set aflame. As both the city and Akaran's mind descend into chaos, only insanity offers rapture.

Book III: Insanity's Reckoning (May 2021)
The most dangerous man in the city is about to get his magic back – and he's got a murder on his mind. As he prepares to hunt a sadistic vampire, his past is about to come back to haunt him in a way he never could have imagined.

Book IV: Insanity's Requiem (Summer 2021)
It's time for the madness to end, but the insane have no desire to find peace –

and peace will only come when Basion City is turned into an open grave.

Origins of the Dead Men Walking
Year 510 of the Queen's Rule
Blind shot (Release date: TBA)
A self-professed Merchant of Secrets enlists the help of the Northern Hunter's Guild to trek to the Cursed Continent of Agromah to recover a relic lost to time. In this land of the dead, what chance does a blind man have against a demon king?

Year 512 of the Queen's Rule
Slag Harbor (An Interruption in the Snowflakes Trilogy)
After battling Makolichi in Gonta – and before facing him down for the final time in Toniki – Akaran decides to leave Private Galagrin behind in the City of Mud to make sure that nothing got missed in his sweep. What he finds is more than just stray shiriak; it's an answer to an unasked question...

Year 513 of the Queen's Rule
Lady Claw I: Claw Unsheathed
Who's to blame when a young girl is accused of murder? Did she do it, or did her father? And when she's cornered and the claws come out... does it matter?

Year 516 of the Queen's Rule
Fearmonger
Years after Toniki, a grizzled Akaran serves as a peacekeeper to the Queen – and nothing wants the peace to be kept.

Year 517 of the Queen's Rule
Blindsided
Stannoth and Elrok couldn't be any more different. Trained mercenaries in the Hunter's Guild, they absolutely hate each other – but they don't have a choice but to work together.

WELCOME TO A WORLD WHERE GOOD THINGS HAPPEN TO BAD PEOPLE
AND THE GOOD PEOPLE ARE QUESTIONABLE...
...AT BEST.

Good things come to those who wait, but I'm impatient as the fires in the Abyss are hot (or cold, depending on Frosel). I'm working on the next book as fast as I can (I promise!) and I've got some stuff for you.

Please be sure to follow me on social media to find out where I'm going, what I'm doing, how I'm doing it, and the occasional stupid meme just to laugh. Plus, get some random business insights on the self-published side of the coin AND see what I'm doing when I dress up for charity purposes.

There's a newsletter you can sign up for!

You can expect free stories, character information, special promotions, extra information about the World of the Saga, and more! Be sure to visit and subscribe (it'd mean a lot to me if you did)!

Amazon.com:
https://www.amazon.com/author/sdmw

Facebook.com:
https://www.facebook.com/sagadmw

Website:
http://www.sagadmw.com

Twitter:
https://www.twitter.com/sagadmw

Instagram:
https://www.twitter.com/sagadmw

Dead Men Emailing Newsletter
http://www.sagadmw.com/email.html

ALSO!
Please don't forget to leave a review. Your opinion on the story (and the series!) MATTERS. Loved it or hated it, thought it was amazing or thought it was garbage, your feedback helps me be a better author and helps me provide the best experience that I can for not just you, but other readers in the future.

Made in the USA
Middletown, DE
04 September 2024

59740382R10057